Praise for *New York Times* bestselling author Rachel Lee

"A mix of angst and humor delivered in a vividly imaginative, soulful narrative."
—*RT Book Reviews* on *A Cowboy for Christmas* (Top Pick!)

"While the relationship-building excels, it is the heroine's strength in the face of such personal adversities that is the real scene-stealer."
—*RT Book Reviews* on *A Conard County Baby*

"Lee's poignant, tragic tale of loss brings to light the suffering of many returning vets; her anguish-filled dialogue makes it real."
—*RT Book Reviews* on *The Widow of Conard County* (Top Pick!, Winner of Best Harlequin Special Edition, 2013)

"A dramatic suspenseful tale about moving forward with your life when interruptions occur."
—*Fresh Fiction* on *Conard County Marine*

"*Defending the Eyewitness* is a page-turner full of mystery and suspense, keeping the reader engaged every step of the way."
—*Fresh Fiction*

Dear Reader,

Sometimes life teaches us to hold everything that is sensitive deep within ourselves. To make ourselves untouchable in order to get by. For Gil, a Green Beret with more than fifteen years in Special Forces, the awful things he's endured, the losses he's suffered, have taught him to keep his guard high. When he comes home to bury a buddy, performing his last official act for Al Baker, he seems like a tower of granite to the heroine, Miriam Baker—Al's cousin.

But he is not granite. He's more like a castle with all the drawbridges raised. When he returns to visit the family, thinking he might be able to tell them things about Al they'll appreciate knowing, he is suffering from a terrible wound, living with pain and doubts about whether he has a future. The granite he appears to be begins to crack. Because, in the end, he is still human, and sometimes the pain just needs to find a way out, and comfort to find a way in.

Happy reading,

Rachel Lee

A Soldier in Conard County

Rachel Lee

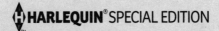

HARLEQUIN® SPECIAL EDITION

ISBN-13: 978-1-335-46555-9

A Soldier in Conard County

Printed in U.S.A.

www.Harlequin.com

Rachel Lee was hooked on writing by the age of twelve and practiced her craft as she moved from place to place all over the United States. This *New York Times* bestselling author now resides in Florida and has the joy of writing full-time.

To all the men and women who have made sacrifices the rest of us can't begin to comprehend. May you find comfort.

Prologue

Followed by a smaller car, the hearse backed up behind Watkins Funeral Home on Poplar Street in Conard City, Wyoming. The old Victorian-style mansion looked fresh in every detail, although buildings around it appeared a little shabby.

As the hearse stopped, the driver climbed out of the following car. Wearing the ASU blue army uniform—dark blue coat and lighter blue slacks with a gold stripe running up the side of them—he stood staring at the nondescript white double doors bearing the discreetly lettered sign Arrivals. His many ribbons gleamed on his chest, and his uniform sported the insignia of the special forces and paratrooper. His upper arm patch ranked him as a sergeant first class; five golden hash marks on the lower sleeve recorded at least fifteen years of service. A brass nameplate identified him as "York." He stood tall and straight, every line of him like a fresh crease.

Then he settled his green beret on his head, squaring it exactly from long experience. The driver exited the hearse and went to knock on the door. Sgt. York had brought home the body of his best buddy, Al Baker, and he intended to ensure that everything was done right.

The funeral director was waiting. Gil York watched as the flag-draped coffin was rolled indoors on a table, then followed when it was moved to a viewing room and placed on a blue-skirted catafalque. There would be no open coffin. If anyone in the family wanted to see, Gil would prevent it. Some things should not be seen.

"I'll notify the family he's here," the funeral director said in a quiet voice.

Sgt. Gil York nodded. "You arranged the honor guard?"

"We have a group of vets in the area who do the honors," the director said.

"The bugler?"

"Sgt. Baker's cousin wants to play 'Taps,'" the director said. "She teaches music at the high school."

From gray eyes that resembled the hard Western mountains, Gil looked at him. "It'll be difficult. It's tough even when it's not your own family."

The director nodded. "I warned her. She insists."

* * *

An hour later, the viewing room began to slowly fill with quiet, sad life. Sgt. York, now wearing white gloves, stood at the foot of the coffin, still at attention, his beret tucked under his arm, surrounded by the flowers the funeral director had arranged. Quiet voices murmured, as if afraid of disturbing the dead.

Gil stared straight ahead, but he wasn't really seeing the room or the people. Instead he was seeing the years he had known Al Baker, filled with dangerous, tense, funny and good memories. His brother-in-arms. His friend through it all.

The flowers reached through his memories, sickeningly sweet. Al wouldn't have liked them. He'd have understood the need for people to send them, but he still wouldn't have liked them.

What he would have liked was the battlefield cross: the empty boots, the nose-down M-16, his green beret resting on the butt. His buddies had planted one for him in the Middle East at their base camp, and Gil had constructed one here, with a variation: he'd covered the rifle butt not with a helmet but with Al's green beret, a symbol they had worked so hard to win and of which they had both been very proud.

One more day, Al, he thought. *Just one more day and you'll be at rest.* No more traveling, no more being shunted all over the world. Peace at last, the peace they had both believed they'd been fighting for all along. Not the right kind of peace, but peace anyway. Gil wasn't sure if there was a heaven. He'd seen too much of hell in his life, but if there was a heaven, he was certain Al was standing post already, free of fear and threats.

His eyes closed for a moment, and Al seemed to stand before him in full dress uniform. Straight and squared away and…smiling.

Godspeed.

The murmuring voices suddenly fell silent. Instantly alert, he turned his head a little and saw a man and woman walking toward the coffin. The woman wore black and leaned heavily on the man's arm.

Al's parents. He recognized them from photos. At once he pivoted so he faced the room and the approaching couple. Al's mother made no attempt to conceal the tears that rolled down her face. His father looked grim, and his jaw worked as he clung to self-control.

The couple approached the flag-covered coffin, and Betsy Baker reached out a hand to touch it. "I want to see him."

Gil tensed, wondering if he would have to warn her off.

The funeral director hurried over and took her hand gently, sparing Gil the necessity. "Please, Betsy."

"I want to see him," she repeated brokenly.

Gil nearly stepped forward. The funeral director spoke first. "No. You don't."

Then Betsy startled Gil. She turned her head, and her brown eyes, so like Al's, locked with his. "You're Gil, aren't you?"

"Yes, ma'am."

"I can't see him?"

Gil broke his rigid posture and went to the woman's side, taking her hand from the funeral director. "Mrs. Baker, Al wouldn't want you to see him now. He'd be very grateful if you didn't. Trust me."

"Sgt. York is right," said Mr. Baker, speaking for the first time. "He's right, Betsy."

The woman squeezed her eyes closed and more huge tears rolled down her face. "All right," she whispered. "All right." Then her voice strengthened. "There's a supper afterward, Gil. Please come. I'm sure Al would like that."

"Yes, ma'am."

Then he resumed his post, rigid as steel, all the barriers back in place. Little could touch him there, and there he remained. Service tomorrow at two. Interment at three. Then back to base.

He'd done this before. He wanted never to do it again.

At graveside the next day, Miriam Baker, Al's younger cousin, stood nervously by the riflemen who were part of the honor guard. She knew most of the guard because they lived in the county, and they'd let her know exactly what to expect and when she was to play her trumpet. They'd bucked her up, too, assuring her she'd do just fine. She wasn't nearly as certain as she pretended to be. Al's loss had carved a hole in her heart that kept tightening her chest at unexpected moments. If that happened while she played "Taps"…

Another car arrived, one she didn't recognize. It stopped in an area away from the gravesite. Then, unfolding from it, was a tall man in army blue, with white gloves on his hands and a green beret that he immediately put on his head. For a moment, he stood surveying the scene: six uniformed pallbearers waiting beside the gravel road. The three riflemen near her.

Gil York. It had to be, even though he hadn't come to the supper last night.

All of a sudden she felt seriously inadequate. The wind whipped her navy-blue concert gown around her lower legs as if trying to pick her up and sweep her away. Only the familiar weight of the trumpet in her hand pinned her to the ground.

Gil York was Al's best friend. Everyone had known in advance that he was bringing Al home. He was also the NCOIC, according to Wade Kendrick and the other vets who had gathered around her extended family in the days since the news arrived. Noncommissioned officer in charge. He would be making sure the entire honor guard did a clean and perfect job.

And then there was her. She could feel his gaze fixate on her. He exchanged salutes with the pallbearers as he passed them, said something that caused them to relax for a moment.

Suddenly, he was standing in front of her, looking as if he'd been carved from granite and put in that dressy uniform. "Ms. Baker," he said. "I'm Gil York."

"I know," she answered, her mouth suddenly dry. "I'm supposed to stand thirty to fifty yards away, right?" Cling to the orders for the day, try not to think too hard about her loss. Everyone's loss.

"That's not as much my concern, ma'am, as you are."

"Me?" Her voice cracked. She was not ordinarily a mouse, but since word had been delivered that Al had been killed, a lot of things seemed to have turned topsy-turvy.

"'Taps' is very difficult to play, Ms. Baker. And I don't mean musically. This is going to be very difficult for you emotionally. If you have any doubt about your ability, let me know. I have the authorized digital recording with me."

Her back stiffened a bit. "It's something I can do for Al. I want to do it. I'll cry later."

Their eyes locked, hers as blue as the summer sky, his as gray as rain-wet slate.

"Very well," he said after a few stretched-out seconds. "If you change your mind, just let me know." Then he turned to the riflemen, who told him they'd already picked out the location for them and for Miri.

Sgt. York approved, saluted and started to pivot away. Suddenly he turned back. "Commander Hardin?"

Seth Hardin, decked out in dark navy blue, smiled faintly. "It's been a while, Sergeant."

"Yes, it has." He nodded, then pivoted and marched away.

There was steel in the man's spine, Miriam thought. She wondered if he ever walked normally, or if he was forever marching, executing tight corners and sharp about-faces.

Not today. Certainly not today.

She and the riflemen backed up to the small knoll Seth Hardin had chosen for them. Thirty to fifty yards from the gravesite for them and the bugler. Apparently, everything was measured out with these formalities.

She only wished she had a real bugle, but the trumpet was acceptable. At least she was sure she could play it.

Events began to blur. The hearse arrived. Family and friends crowded into the chairs that had been set up at the gravesite. The grave itself was covered by the machinery that would lower Al into his resting place later. For now, everything was hidden beneath a blanket of artificial turf, shockingly green against the duller, dry countryside.

Then she heard commands being barked. The moment had come. Six men in uniforms of various services eased the coffin from the back of the hearse and carried her cousin with measured steps to the grave.

Miri's throat tightened until she felt as if a wire garrote wrapped it. She drew slow breaths, calming herself. Weeping could come later. She had a service to perform for Al.

The minister spoke a few words, led them in a prayer. Then Sgt. York turned toward the distant riflemen and saluted. Even though she stood ten yards from them, Miri could hear the snap as they brought their rifles up and aimed them to the sky.

A command was spoken and three rifle volleys rang out, one after the other. Then, with a snap, the rifles returned to a position that crossed the men's chests.

She glanced toward York and saw him waiting at attention. Her turn. She lifted the trumpet and began playing the sorrowful notes for Al. A hush seemed to come over the entire world. She didn't notice that tears ran down her cheeks. Had no way to tell that no eyes were dry as the lonesome call carried over the countryside.

She made it all the way through. Tears nearly blinded her as the pallbearers stepped forward, folding the flag with perfect precision before handing it to Sgt. York. He pivoted sharply and walked to stand directly before Al's parents. With the flag at waist height he bent forward and spoke, his determined voice carrying on the stirring breeze.

"On behalf of the president of the United States, the United States Army and a grateful nation, please accept this flag as a symbol of our appreciation for your loved one's honorable and faithful service."

Mrs. Baker took the flag and held it to her chest, her sobs becoming audible.

Then the entire honor guard withdrew, leaving the family to its private time of grief.

Something made Miri run, her trumpet case banging against her leg. She didn't run away, but rather straight to Sgt. York, who was about to climb into his car.

"Sergeant!" she called. Her voice sounded disturbingly loud, but she didn't care. He'd been Al's friend. These moments were for him, too.

He paused, then pivoted to face her. Still the stern-faced soldier. "Yes, ma'am?" he asked quietly when she reached him.

"You can't just go. Please at least let us know how to contact you. Al's stories…well, we feel like you're part of the family, too."

He hesitated a moment. "Do you have a pad and pen? There's very little I can fit into a dress uniform without looking sloppy."

"I imagine." She was in a luckier position. Her trumpet case contained the paper and pen. He scribbled down an email address. Nothing more. It was enough. "Thank you. Thank you for everything."

"No need. Al deserved a whole lot more." Then he opened the car door and removed a paper-wrapped parcel, the size of a large book. "Give this to Al's mother and father, please. I had a bunch of photos I thought they'd like. I was going to mail it but… You did well, Ms. Baker."

Then he climbed in the car and, like the rest of the honor guard, disappeared from sight.

Miri stood holding the wrapped package, sorrow and loss emptying her heart. She missed Al like the devil. But she suspected Gil York missed him even more.

Chapter One

Miri Baker waited nervously. Gil York was arriving sometime this evening. Yes, they'd kept up a casual email correspondence since Al's funeral last year, but then he'd dropped out of sight for over two months.

When he resurfaced he'd told her he'd been wounded and that, after rehab, he'd be going home to his family in Michigan.

She wondered what had happened there, because out of the blue, just a week ago, he'd asked if the family would mind a visit from him. After clearing it with Al's parents, she assured him they'd love it, and his response had been brief. "See you Friday evening."

In the few messages they'd traded since he told her he'd been wounded, there had been a lot of blanks, missing lines, little information. She had no idea what to expect, or why he'd leave his family and come here.

She had a casserole ready to go, since his arrival time was up in the air. She had some lesson planning to do, but it could wait. She paced her small house and hoped that everything would be all right.

She had no idea how badly wounded Gil had been. What was he going to say when he learned that Al's family was throwing a big barbecue for him tomorrow? A barbecue in January because of a brief thaw. He wouldn't be expecting that. What if he didn't want to go?

"Simple enough," Betsy, Al's mother, had said as she gave her phone a workout. "We'll have the barbecue anyway. Everyone will have a good time." Especially since no one thought of holding barbecues at this time of year, thaw or no thaw. In a pinch, the barn would do for shelter.

It was nearly a year since the funeral, and when Miri thought over the simple, short emails she and Gil had exchanged, she felt that now he was even more a stranger than he had been when Al had shared stories about him.

"Reserved" might be an understatement when describing Gil York. From the little she had seen of him at the funeral, she would now describe him as distant. Maybe even closed off. She had a feeling that during their brief meeting she'd had her first close encounter with what she'd heard called the "thousand-yard stare."

She'd talked about it with Edie Hardin, a former

combat search and rescue pilot who now worked for the county's emergency medical services as a helicopter pilot. The woman had a son who had frequent play dates with Miri's next-door neighbor's son, and Edie and Miri had developed a friendship over time.

"I know what you mean," Edie had answered. "I've seen it plenty of times." She had missed the funeral because she was on duty that day, but her husband, Seth, a former SEAL, had been part of the honor guard.

"I see it in Seth sometimes," Edie had continued. "What these guys do? Especially special forces like Seth and Gil...so much, for so long. It's like a brain shock, or an emotional shock. It haunts them, Miri. Anyway, don't worry about it. Gil seems to have a handle on it, from what you said."

Handle on it? Truth be told she was surprised he'd continued their irregular email conversation. Little said on his side, while she tried to pass along interesting tidbits about life around here. She kept expecting him to just not answer.

Then for two months he hadn't. It had been a shock to *her* to learn he'd been wounded and that he was on indefinite medical leave. An even bigger shock when he'd written that he'd like to visit, if that was all right.

Of course it was all right. He'd been Al's best friend for years. By extension he was family. But what about his own family, where he'd been headed when he first told her he was wounded?

As the sun slipped behind the mountains and the afternoon began to darken into twilight, she decided she was getting entirely too anxious about Gil's visit. He was probably just taking the opportunity to do a little traveling while he was on leave. He undoubtedly knew people from all over the country and was catching up. Considering that Al had been one of his best buddies, he probably wondered how the Baker family was getting along.

Losing Al still hurt. Grief, she was discovering, never really lessened; it just came less often. Like ocean waves, rolling over her occasionally, sometimes softer, sometimes hammering. Talking with his parents, she'd found they were experiencing the same thing, only much more painfully. Their only child? Indescribable.

The folded flag took pride of place beside Al's official portrait on the Bakers' mantel over the fireplace. Around it were all the presentation cases holding Al's medals, and a white votive candle that was never allowed to go out. Miri had offered recently to get all the medals mounted and framed—an expensive proposition, to her surprise—but they hadn't decided yet.

The Baker family continued to move forward with life, because that was what the living had to do, but Miri couldn't escape the feeling that part of Betsy, and maybe Jack, as well, had been frozen in time, at the moment they'd learned of Al's death.

Jack was still running the ranch; his grief didn't diminish realities. Yet some light in him was gone.

Maybe that was what was going on with Gil. Some light had been extinguished. Well, how would it be possible to spend sixteen or more years fighting for your country on dangerous and covert missions, without a bit of your internal light going out?

Then she realized why she was so on edge, and it had little to do with Gil personally. It had to do with the concern that his visit was going to freshen a grief they all, particularly Al's parents, had been gradually learning to live with.

Outside, the January thaw had thinned the snow to almost nothing. Icicles were beginning to drop from the eaves, tiny spears for the most part, probably a good size for leprechauns.

The day faded rapidly toward early night. Miri hated waiting, but she couldn't seem to do anything else just then. Finally, after what seemed like forever, a dark-colored car pulled up out front. A few minutes later she recognized the unmistakable figure of Gil York.

He looked different out of uniform, wearing a black parka, and as he came around the front of the car, she realized everything about him had changed.

The ramrod-straight posture and confident movement she associated with him were gone. He walked a bit gingerly, using a cane. He wore laced-up desert boots and camouflage pants beneath the parka, an odd assortment of pieces, and she wondered if the camo was simply comfortable, preferred over jeans or regular slacks.

He caught sight of her as she opened the door and gave a small wave. She noticed how deliberate his pace remained and the caution with which he navigated the sidewalk and the porch steps.

"It's good to see you again, Gil," she said when he reached the porch. She noted that sweat had beaded on his forehead, and it wasn't an especially warm day, thaw or not. That walk must have been difficult.

"Come inside. I've got coffee if you want, and a casserole that's just waiting to be popped in the oven."

At last the rigid lines of his face cracked a bit, serving up a faint smile. "Thank you, Miri. Hard to believe that I sat through that long drive and I'm already looking for another seat."

"You've been wounded," she replied, stating the obvious. "It must take time to come back." She opened the door wider and motioned him inside. Her house was small, the foyer about big enough for four people, with the living room on one side and the kitchen on the other. At least the kitchen was big enough to eat in. Two bedrooms and a bath at the back. Cozy. Easy to make crowded.

Gil was a large enough man that he was making her house feel even smaller. She guided him straight to the kitchen and pulled out a chair for him at the battered wooden table, which doubled as food prep space when she needed it. While he removed his parka, revealing a loden-green chamois shirt, she asked, "Coffee?"

"Please. Black."

She placed a large mug in front of him, then slipped the casserole into the oven, which she had preheated more than an hour ago. That freed her to join him at the table.

"I was surprised when you said you wanted to visit," she remarked. "Everyone's glad you are, we just didn't expect it. Was the trip rough?"

Again the faintest of smiles. "It's a long way from Michigan by car. Some really great scenery, though. Mostly, it was peaceful."

There was something important in the way he said that, but she felt she shouldn't ask, not yet. He had an aura that made her feel getting personal might not be wise. That he didn't easily allow it, if he did at all.

"How are Al's parents?" he asked.

"One day at a time. Jack's still running the ranch, although I think his heart has gone out of it. He planned to turn it over to Al when he left the army. Now it's just something he needs to do. He's muttered a couple of times that maybe he can find a Japanese buyer."

Gil arched one dark brow. "Japanese?"

"Oh, that goes back a couple of decades at least. The Japanese were buying up cattle ranches in Montana, then having locals run them, so they could export the beef to Japan. I guess it was pricey there."

"It's pricey everywhere now."

"Not that the ranchers are seeing most of that."

He nodded. "I didn't think so. Al used to talk about the ranch on occasion. Stories from when he was a kid, mostly, but he always had something to share when he came back from leave. And he was always pushing me to join him when we retired."

"Did you want to?"

His eyes were like flint, showing only the faintest of expressions. "What do I know about ranching?"

That finally caused her to smile. "What did you know about special ops when you started?"

"Touché." At last a real smile from him. So his expressions could change from distant to less distant, to even pleasant. He lifted his mug at last and drank deeply of the coffee. "Great joe," he told her.

"Thanks. Listen, I've got a spare bedroom in the back, if you don't mind that it has my home office in one corner. I can guarantee, though, that it's nicer than the motel. And tomorrow Betsy and Jack are looking forward to seeing you." She hesitated. "They're throwing a barbecue for you."

"A barbecue?" He raised one brow. "It's January."

"And there's a thaw. Everyone's looking forward to an early taste of spring. Anyway, you're not obligated to come, but if you do you'll get to meet some of Al's old friends."

He didn't answer and she really didn't expect him to. He'd asked if it would be all right to come for a brief visit, not to be swamped.

After a few minutes, realizing that even their email exchanges hadn't really made them more than acquaintances, she spoke again. "You can bring your stuff in whenever you're ready. Dinner will be in about an hour. And you can think about just what you want out of this visit. In the meantime, after that drive, maybe you need a nap?"

His gaze had grown distant, but it snapped back to her as she spoke. It was a penetrating look, and she didn't doubt that she had his full attention.

"I'm sorry," he said. "Yes, I'm tired. Yes, I'm still recovering. But the thing that wore me out most was my own family."

She drew a breath. His *own* family? Oh, Lord, and she'd just suggested a big barbecue with Al's friends and family. Gil was probably already wishing he hadn't stopped by. "What happened?" she asked, before she could stop herself.

"For years now they've been demanding I get out of the military. My being wounded only strengthened it. They always feared I was going to come home in a body bag, and this time I came close. My dad's a Vietnam vet, and he's been pushing the hardest."

"Oh." She'd heard the same insistence from Betsy and Jack when Al came home. "Jack used to ask Al, 'How many years, son? You've done your duty.'"

Gil nodded slightly. "Part of me understands. I've buried a lot of good men. I've seen a lot of terrible things. But this is who I am."

It sounded like a line drawn in the sand. Being a soldier was his identity. How did you strip that away? She would find it hard to give up being a music teacher. Sometimes she wondered how jobs could become so overwhelmingly important to a sense of self. Wondering didn't make it change.

"I'm not sure you'll get much of that here," she said. "But I can't guarantee you won't get any. Al's parents are excited about seeing you because Al mentioned you so often they feel like you're family. So, no promises."

Again a faint smile. "I know how to leave. Obviously. But let's talk about you. I know you teach music. I know you love it because you told me such great stories when you emailed. But what about the rest? Does Miri Baker have a life apart from school?"

She narrowed her eyes at him. "Does Sergeant Gil York have a life apart from the Green Berets?" Then she laughed. "Of course I have a life. Friends. Community service projects. Sometimes I help Jack and Betsy at the ranch. There are times when they need some extra hands."

"And your parents? Al never mentioned them. At least not that I can recall."

She closed her eyes. Even after seven years she didn't like to think about it. "My dad had an accident with some farm machinery. Mom found him... It was gruesome. Anyway, she died of a sudden heart attack before the EMTs arrived. I'm glad she didn't have to hang around, but I resent it, too." That was blunt enough, she thought.

"So you were left to deal with it alone?"

"Hardly," she said a touch drily. "You're forgetting the rest of the Baker clan. Aunt Betsy and Uncle Jack were there for me, as were a couple of more distant cousins. Then there are the people around here. Unless you deliberately push them away, quite a few will try to be helpful however they can."

He didn't answer immediately. He looked so very

different from when he'd come for the funeral. Then he'd been rigid, sturdy, in control. Now he looked weary, new lines creased his strong features and his eyes weren't quite as flinty. She wondered if he was in much pain, but didn't ask. They were still virtual strangers, with little enough intimacy of any kind. It was like meeting someone new, their past contact irrelevant. For some reason she hadn't expected that.

He rose from the table, moving as if he was stiff and uncomfortable, and the change once again shocked her. He poured himself more coffee, then returned to his seat. He'd managed without the cane, however.

"I stiffen up when I sit too long," he remarked. "I didn't use to do that. Al talked about you a lot."

The switch in topics caught her by surprise. She'd begun to hope he was going to say something about himself, but now went back to Al.

"I miss him," she said. "Even though he was home only a few weeks a year, I still miss him."

"I think he missed you, too. We were sitting behind some rocks one cold night keeping watch, and he told me about how you used to build roads together in the dirt at the ranch. And how you always wanted mountains, so you'd find some rocks, but you were very critical about them. Some were too rounded. Others didn't look like the mountains you can see from here."

She smiled at the memory. "I drove him crazy with my mountains. He had a toy grader and was making roads fast, to run the little cars and trucks on, but I was wandering around trying to make mountains. Then my folks got me a couple of plastic horses and they were too big. I hate to tell you how many times they turned into monsters that messed with the tiny cars."

Gil's face relaxed into a smile. "I can imagine it."

Her thoughts drifted backward in time, and she found herself remembering the happiness almost wistfully. "We tried to build a tree fort but we really didn't have the skills, so we'd climb up into the trees and pretend to be hiding from unspecified bad guys. One time we happened to find a stray steer. Well, that ended our imaginary game. We had to take it home. For which we got a piece of cake, so after that instead of hiding from imaginary bad guys, we became trackers hunting for rustled cattle."

His smile widened. "He didn't tell me you two had hunted rustlers."

"Only in our minds. Kids have wonderful imaginations. So what did you do?"

"I lived in town, so most of our games were pretty tame. Except when we got into trouble, of course. And being kids, we did from time to time. Mrs. Green was pretty angry when we trampled her rhubarb bed."

"I can imagine."

"Oh, it came back. We weren't trying to do any damage, though. Just carelessness. I haven't been home a lot during my career, but it seems like kids don't run around the neighborhood as much as they used to. Yards have become more private."

"And with two parents working, a lot of kids are probably in after-school programs and day care."

"True." He sipped some more coffee.

"When did you start thinking about joining the army?" she asked. "Or did you imagine a series of different possibilities?"

"I don't remember if I thought about anything else seriously. I probably toyed with a lot of ideas, the way kids do. Then September 11 happened. That was it."

"Pretty much the same thing happened with Al. That set his course."

"Yup." Gil nodded slowly. "It set a lot of courses. I trained with a whole bunch of people who'd made the same decision for the same reason. The changing of a nation."

She turned that around in her mind. "Watershed?" she asked tentatively.

"In a lot of ways." But he clearly intended to say no more about it. "And you? Music teacher?"

"Always. Put any musical instrument in my hand and I wanted to play it. I was lucky, because Mom and Dad encouraged me even though it was expensive. Rented instruments and band fees. Then I got a scholarship to the music program at university."

"You must be very talented."

"Talented enough to teach. Nothing wrong with that. I never did dream of orchestras or bands." She smiled. "Small dreams."

"Big dreams," he corrected. "Teaching is a big dream."

As she watched, she could see fatigue pulling him down. His eyelids were growing heavy and caffeine wasn't doing a bit to help. "Why don't you take a nap," she suggested. "I'll wake you for dinner, but you looked wiped."

He didn't argue, merely gave her a wan smile and let her show him the bedroom in back. His limp, she noticed, had grown even more pronounced than when he came into the house. Tired and hurting. She hoped he'd sleep.

Gil didn't sleep. He pulled off his boots, then stretched out carefully on the colorful quilt that covered the twin bed on one side of the room. As Miri had advised him, her home office occupied one corner. An older computer occupied most of the desk, but there was a side table stacked high with papers, and leaning against it was a backpack that looked to be full. Several instrument cases lined the wall on the far side.

He still wasn't sure exactly what had drawn him here, unless it was memories of Al. He *had* needed to get away from his family, all of whom were pushing him to take medical retirement. He didn't feel right about that. He might be confined to a desk after this— hell, probably would—but he still had buddies in the unit, and even from a desk he could look out for them. He owed them something, just as he owed something to all the friends he'd lost over the years.

His family had trouble understanding that. Even his dad, who was a Vietnam vet. Of course, he had taken only one tour in that war before his enlistment finished, so maybe he couldn't understand, either. A deep bond grew between men in special forces, no matter the branch they served in. They were used more often on dangerous and covert missions, often so far removed from command that they might as well have been totally alone. They depended on each other for everything.

And they wound up owing each other everything. Didn't mean they all liked each other, but they were brothers, the bond deeper than most families.

How could he possibly explain that?

So…he'd finally gotten tired of the pressure. His mind was made up. He'd made his choice the day he entered training for special ops, and a wounding, even his second one, couldn't change that commitment.

But the real problem was that he and his family were no longer on the same page. They couldn't be. His folks had no real understanding of where he'd been and what he'd done, and he wasn't going to try to illuminate them. They had no need to know, and the telling wasn't the same as the doing, anyway. He was part of a different world, and sometimes he felt as if they were speaking different languages.

It was a kind of isolation that only being with others who'd been in special ops could break. They had become his family, his only real family now. How the hell could he explain that to his parents?

He couldn't. So he'd put up with their fussing and pressure as long as he could. They wanted to take care of him, they worried about him and they couldn't just accept who he was. Not their fault, but in the end he didn't feel the comfort they wanted him to feel.

Al had been a good reason to move on. Gil told his folks he wanted to come see Al's family, to see how they were doing, to share stories about Al they'd probably like to hear. That was one decision that hadn't received an argument. Maybe because his parents were as tired of trying to break down his walls as he was at having them battered.

He wasn't accustomed to the kind of weariness that had become part of his life since he got caught in a bomb blast in the mountains of Afghanistan. Yeah, he'd gotten tired from lack of sleep in the past, but this was different. Fatigue had become a constant companion, so he let his eyes close.

And behind his eyelids all he could see was Miriam Baker and her honeyed hair in its cute braid. If she meant to look businesslike, she wasn't succeeding.

A thought slipped past his guard: *sexy woman.* Al probably wouldn't want him to notice. Then Gil could no longer hold sleep at bay.

Miri used the time while Gil napped to call her aunt and uncle. Betsy answered.

"He's here," Miriam said. "He looks awful, Betsy. Worn-out, pale, and he's got a bad limp. I don't know if he's up to the barbecue tomorrow. He hasn't said."

"If he comes," Betsy said firmly, "all he needs to do is sit in one of the Adirondack chairs and hold court. Looks like it'll be warm enough to be outdoors, but we're opening the barn so folks can get out of the wind if they need to. He'll be cozy in there."

"And if he doesn't want to come?"

"Then we'll come visit him when he feels more like it."

Miri paused, thinking, and for the first time it struck her that Betsy had used news of Gil's arrival to create a huge distraction for herself. Throwing together a large barbecue on a week's notice was no easy task, and it probably didn't leave much time for anything else…such as grieving. This barbecue wasn't for Gil.

She felt a little better then. She wouldn't have to try to pressure Gil in some way if he didn't want to go, and considering how worn he looked, he probably wouldn't. But Betsy would have achieved what she needed, a week when she was busy from dawn to dusk planning something happy.

Life on a ranch in the winter could often be isolated. Too cold to go out; the roads sometimes too bad to even go grocery shopping. This January thaw was delivering more than warm temperatures. Miri almost smiled into the phone.

"I asked him to stay in my spare room," she told her aunt. "He hasn't answered. He might prefer to go to the motel."

"Well, he's probably slept in a lot of worse places."

"By far," Miri agreed, chuckling. Both of them remembered some of Al's stories about sitting in the mouth of a cave, no fire, no warm food, colder than something unmentionable, until he was off watch and could lie down on cold rock. Yeah, Gil had slept in far worse places than the La-Z-Rest Motel, which was at least clean and heated.

"So," she asked her aunt, "are you ready for tomorrow? Do I need to bring anything beyond a ton of potato salad and two dozen burger buns?"

Betsy's tone grew humorous. "Considering that everyone is insisting on bringing something, we'll probably have more food than anyone can eat. It's been a struggle to ensure we don't just get forty pies."

Miri laughed. "That's about right. So you marshaled everyone into shape?"

"Better believe it. Plus extra gas grills and the manly chefs to cook on them."

Another giggle escaped Miri. "Manly chefs?"

"You don't suppose any woman in this county has let her husband know that she could grill a burger or dog as well as he can? It's a guy thing."

Miri pressed her lips together, stifling more laughter. She needed to take care not to wake Gil. But her aunt was funny.

"I've decided," Betsy said, "that manning charcoal and gas grills has become the substitute for hunting the food for the tribe."

"Oh, that's not fair," Miri insisted. "Most of the men around here go hunting."

"Sure. And most aren't all that successful. Once the masses of armed men hit the woods and mountains, wise animals pick up stakes and move away."

Miri was delighted to hear her aunt's sense of

humor surfacing again. Not since word of Al's death had Betsy achieved more than a glimmer of humor. Now she was bubbling over with it. Miri could have blessed Gil for deciding to visit. And she began to suspect it wasn't just arranging this barbecue that had lifted Betsy's spirits.

Maybe, Miri thought after they said goodbye, it had helped in some way to know that Al's best friend hadn't forgotten him. A reassurance of some kind? Or a connection that hadn't been lost?

Miri guessed she'd never figure out exactly what was going on with Betsy, but somehow she'd needed this visit from Gil.

And maybe Gil had needed it just as much. He certainly needn't have come all the way out here to people he'd never met until a funeral, people he'd barely met before he left.

All she knew was that she herself hadn't wanted to lose touch with Al's friend, even though they were strangers.

Connections, she thought. Connections for them all through a mutual loved one. In that context everything made sense.

Gil didn't sleep long. Years on dangerous missions had taught him to sleep like a cat, and his wounding had only made it more obvious. Fatigued though he was, pain broke through even the deepest sleep.

The fatigue wasn't sleepiness, anyway. The docs had warned him it was going to last awhile, because of how much healing he needed to do. His body was going to sap his energy in order to put him back together. Mostly. Some parts of him would never be the same.

Even back here, through a closed bedroom door, he could smell the aroma of whatever casserole Miri was cooking. Courtesy required him to get up and not keep her waiting for her own dinner.

But the first minutes upon awakening tested him, even though physical discomfort was no stranger. What was it some road cyclist had said? *You need to love pain to do this.* That applied to the kind of work Gil did, as well, although loving pain had little to do with it. You didn't have to be masochistic, you just had to not care.

But somehow he cared during the first couple minutes upon awakening. Maybe because the pain served no real purpose except to make it difficult to move.

Difficult or not, he forced himself to sit up and put his stockinged feet on the floor. He sucked air through his teeth and closed his eyes as angry waves washed through him, as stiffness and discomfort hampered him. He'd been wounded once before. It was part of the job. But this useless response afterward annoyed him. Hampering his movements did no good, not for his body, not for anything.

Because he needed to move. How many times had he been reminded not to let scar tissue tighten up? Hell.

He shoved himself to his feet and grabbed the cane he'd hooked over the back of the office chair. Time to march forth. Time to ease stiffness into a beast he could control, rather than the other way around.

His first few steps were uncertain as he tested his legs' response to walking. Okay. Slow but okay. They screamed at him, but it was a familiar scream now. The burn scars, the skin grafts, they all had an opinion about this. His shattered hip functioned, but not happily. His back didn't think he should stand upright.

Hah. He'd show them.

He opened the door and made his way down the short hallway. The bathroom was on his right, he noticed, marking the terrain. He'd had too little to drink during his drive today. He should remedy that soon.

The kitchen would have been easy to find even if he hadn't already visited it. Delicious aromas would have drawn him with his eyes blindfolded.

Miri sat at the big kitchen table, a stack of papers in front of her. She looked up with a smile. "I thought you'd sleep longer."

"I never sleep long," he answered. "Dinner smells amazing."

"My famous chicken-and-rice casserole. Have a seat. Do you want something to drink?"

"I need to move a bit. But a huge honking glass of water would be wonderful."

She rose at once. "Ice?"

That startled something approaching a laugh from him, and he watched her smile and raise her eyebrows. "Ice is funny?"

"Only if you ever spent months wishing your cave

would warm up. Just water, please. I didn't drink enough on the drive."

"Why not?"

"Because I wanted to avoid getting out of the car for anything other than gas."

He watched her face grow shadowed, then she went to a cupboard and pulled out a tall glass. "You're really hurting badly?"

"It'll pass." His mantra. He wouldn't admit any more than that, anyway.

As he stood there leaning on his cane, she passed him a full glass of delicious water. He drained it unceremoniously, and she refilled it for him immediately. He sucked half of it down, then placed the glass on the table. "Thanks. Mind if I stretch a bit by walking around the house?"

"Be my guest. Dinner's still fifteen minutes away. Longer if you need. Casseroles keep."

Nice lady, he thought as he began to explore the parameters of her house and his ability to move through it. Small place. Some would call it cozy. She'd certainly dressed it up in pleasant colors. Feminine, in shades of lavender and pale blue, with silky-looking curtains and upholstered chairs and a love seat in similar colors. Her kitchen was a contrast in soft yellows. He hadn't really noticed what she'd done with the guest room–office. He imagined she must have taken years to do all this, given a teacher's salary.

But contrasts were striking him. Everywhere he'd gone, he'd seen how people had tried to create some kind of beauty even when they had few resources. A home like this would look like a palace to many.

Then he remembered Nepal, a country full of rocky mountains, dangerous trails, sparse vegetation and racing rivers. The countryside itself was a thing of beauty, but then you went inside a home or teahouse, and the brilliant colors could take your breath away. Wherever possible, every inch of wall had been covered with bright paintings and cloths, a buttress against the granite and glaciers outside. A statement. A psychological expression: this is home. Beauty created by some of the most welcoming people he'd ever met.

He'd found it much the same when he'd slipped across the border into Tibet to collect intelligence, although the Chinese takeover had managed to wipe out some of the brightness, mainly on the faces of the Tibetans. They still wanted their country back.

Drawing himself out of memory, assisted by fresh pain, he tried to minimize his limp as he returned to the kitchen. Limping only made everything else hurt, too. Damned if he did, damned if he didn't. The saga of life.

Miri was serving up her casserole on large plates. "Hungry?" she asked. "I imagine you didn't eat much if you weren't stopping for water."

"I'm starving," he admitted. "Thanks for asking me to dinner."

She raised a brow and lifted one corner of her mouth. "Do you think I was going to let you arrive after a trip like that and not ply you with food? Seems unneighborly."

Again he felt his face trying to thaw. He didn't want to let it. Showing emotion could be weakening. When he was leading men he could joke, he could get angry, but he couldn't go much beyond showing them he'd do everything in his power to get them back alive.

He also admitted it was a form of self-protection. If you didn't feel it, it couldn't hurt you. Straightforward enough.

But now he was among people who had a whole different metric for dealing with life. Only look at Al's cousin, her readiness to welcome him into her home, her offering him dinner, a place to stay.

It wasn't unusual. He'd met that kind of courtesy the world over, unless people were terrified. There was no reason to be terrified here in Conard County, Wyoming. He felt a vain wish that he could have sprinkled that kind of safety around the whole world. Instead, all he'd ever been able to do was chip away at threats… and sometimes make them worse.

He eased into the chair and balanced his cane against the wall.

"So," she said, "I invited you to stay here." A heaping plate of chicken and rice appeared in front of him. "Say you will, because I'm going to feel just awful if you go to the motel."

He looked up as she brought her own plate to the table, then set the casserole dish nearby in case either of them wanted more. "Why would you feel awful?"

"Because you're Al's friend. Because my office-slash-bedroom is marginally better than the motel. I can guarantee you no bedbugs, not that the motel gets them for lack of sanitation. Some of the people passing through…"

A jug of water joined the casserole dish, and at last she quit buzzing and sat across from him.

He arched a brow. "You think I've never met a bedbug?"

Her expression turned into a mixture of amusement and disgust. "I suppose you have."

"Of course, that doesn't mean I like sharing my bed with them. But we have to get impervious to a lot of things."

"I'd guess so," she said after a moment. "Are you saying I'm squeamish?"

He liked the way humor suddenly lit her blue eyes. "No. You're a product of where you live. Most bugs probably stay outside."

"I have a rule," she answered as she picked up a fork. "If a critter is outside I'm happy to leave it alone. If it comes inside, I'll kill it."

"Seems like a sensible arrangement."

"I love nature," she said, almost laughing. "Outdoors, where it belongs. Please, start eating. If you don't like it, let me know."

"Is it hot?"

"Very."

"Great. That's all I ask."

Meals in the hospital had usually been lukewarm

by the time they reached him. He'd developed a strong loathing for oatmeal that would have made a great wallpaper paste. The mess hall was better but, since army cooks had been replaced by private contractors, not what he remembered from the past. As for when he was in the field…

"One of the best meals I can remember eating," he said as memory awoke, "was in a teahouse in Nepal."

She looked up from her plate. "Nepal? What were you doing there?"

"Passing through. I can't tell you any more than that. But they plied us with hot soup full of fresh vegetables, and roasted yak meat and yak milk. And an amazing amount of hot tea. Those people had next to nothing, Miri, but they treated us like kings."

"They sound very welcoming."

He almost smiled. "I'll never forget them. Strangers in a strange land, and we were met with smiles, generosity and genuine welcome." He looked down and scooped up more casserole. "I've noticed in my travels that the most generous people are often those who have the least. By no standard measure would you think the Nepalese were wealthy. But they were wealthy in soul and spirit."

He emptied his plate in short order and Miri pushed the casserole dish toward him. "I'm not counting on leftovers. Eat, Gil."

He was happy to oblige. Hot meals were still a treat.

"From what Al used to talk about, I guess you've seen a whole lot of the world."

He raised his gaze, feeling himself grow steely again. Some matters were not to be discussed with civilians. "Not from a tourist perspective," he said, closing the subject. A subject he'd opened himself, talking about Nepal. But it needed to be closed.

She nodded slowly, her blue eyes sweeping over his face. "Stay here tonight," she said finally. "You can decide about the barbecue tomorrow."

He was content to leave it there.

Chapter Two

Morning arrived, still dark, but already promising a beautiful day. Miri made pancakes and eggs for breakfast. The tall stack of cakes disappeared fast, with much appreciation from Gil.

"Do you cook?" she asked eventually, making idle conversation over coffee before she cleared the table.

"Over an open fire I'm passable. A can of paraffin even better." He shook his head a little. "When we could, anyway. At base camp we often took turns cooking for each other, but my efforts weren't especially appreciated."

She smiled. "So you got out of it?"

"Often as not. Whatever the knack is, I missed it."

She rose, took the plates to the counter and looked

at the thermometer outside her window. Sunshine had begun to spill over the eastern mountains, brightening the morning.

"It's going to be a beautiful day," she remarked. "The forecast said we're going to reach the upper sixties, and we're already at sixty-one. A great day for a midwinter barbecue."

She waited, wondering if he'd respond to the open invitation about the barbecue, but he said nothing. He sipped coffee, his gaze faraway, and she admitted at last that this guy wasn't about to share much of himself. Safe little tidbits here and there, but no more. Or maybe, despite the passage of time, he was still somewhere else, perhaps the place he'd been wounded. She couldn't imagine the difficulty he must experience transitioning between worlds. Maybe it was never easy. Perhaps it was harder under these circumstances.

She spoke, daring herself to ask. "Does your body feel like a stranger to you?"

One brow lifted. "How did you guess?"

"Well, it just crossed my mind. You're used to being in top physical form. That's gone now, at least for a while. You must be frustrated."

"Not exactly the word I'd choose, but it'll do. Let me help as much as I can with the dishes. I need to be moving."

"Betsy said you could settle in and hold court today if you come." Miri waited, nearly holding her breath.

"I'll go," he said after a minute, then pushed his chair back. "But I doubt I'll hold court. Not my style."

He managed to wash all the dishes and put them in the drain rack without any assistance from her. She had to admit to enjoying watching a man scrub her dishes while she sipped a second cup of coffee.

He was a good-looking man, too. Not as ramrod straight and stiff as at the funeral, which had been kind of intimidating. This version of Gil looked a whole lot more relaxed and approachable. Even if it was discomfort causing it.

When at last he dried his hands and returned to the table, she noticed the fine sheen of sweat on his forehead. "You did too much," she said instantly.

"I did very little, and it'll do me no good to sit on my duff and stiffen up. Don't worry about me. I won't push my limits too far. This isn't some kind of contest."

Firmly but kindly put in her place. The man didn't want anyone worrying about him. Okay then. She could manage that. She couldn't even feel slightly offended. This was a spark of the man she'd seen at the funeral. She was glad to know he was still in there. Living around here, it was possible to get to know veterans who had a lot of trouble returning. She supposed it was unlikely that Gil wouldn't have any problems as a result of his wounding and time at war, but she hoped they were minimal.

"You must still be missing Al," he remarked.

"Yes. You?"

"Damn near every day. You know, even when

you're in the midst of the most dangerous situations imaginable, you don't believe the bad stuff's going to happen to *you*."

"How could you?" she asked. "You'd be paralyzed."

"Maybe. What I do know is that we don't think about it until it's shoved into our faces, like when Al was killed, and then we have to shove it back into a lockbox. Anyway, he had plans. I was supposed to come here with him and help with the family ranch. I guess I told you that."

Gil was rambling a little, she thought, but no more than most people in casual conversation. At least he was talking.

"Al," he said again. "Damn. Ever the optimist. He could find a reason to be happy about cold beans on a subzero night."

That was Al. That was definitely the Al she remembered. "I take it you're not as much of an optimist?"

"Maybe I was, too much, anyway. Doesn't matter. Here we are." He gave her a faint, almost apologetic smile.

"Are you going back to duty?" she dared to ask.

"Yes."

There was a firmness to the way he said the word that again suggested a line had been drawn in the sand. "Do you have any idea when?"

"Not yet. Probably as soon as they feel I'm well enough to play desk jockey for an eight- or twelve-hour day."

"So...you won't be going back into the field?"

"No." A single uncompromising word. A warning to back off.

She could have sighed, except she knew she had no right to be asking many questions. He'd wanted to come out here for some reason...and she suspected it wasn't just to tell the family amusing stories about Al. All she'd done was offer him a bed and a few meals. He didn't owe her anything, certainly not answers to questions he might consider to be prying.

Apparently, he must have caught something in her expression. Much as she schooled herself to keep a straight face when necessary, because her young students picked up on even the subtlest of clues, she must have just failed. He spoke.

"Sorry to be so abrupt."

"It's okay," she said swiftly. "You're not feeling well..."

"Feeling unwell has nothing to do with it. Months of arguing with my family does. I'm not retiring, much as they may want me to, and if I can get back into shape for the field I will."

Now she wondered if getting away from his family had been his primary reason for traveling this way. "Families are harder to handle than combat missions?"

He astonished her by cracking an unexpected laugh. "Are you suggesting I turned tail?"

"I don't believe I said that."

For the first time she saw a spark of something in

those flinty eyes. Heat? Humor? She couldn't read it. "No, you didn't. What time is this barbecue and what can I do to help?"

Because night fell so early in the winter, the barbecue had been planned for midday. By noon, Miri had two huge containers of potato salad in the back of her sport SUV, along with four paper bags full of hamburger buns. There'd be leftovers, but she was sure they wouldn't go to waste.

She hesitated, wondering if she should tell Gil to follow her or invite him to ride with her. If he had his own vehicle he could leave whenever he wanted. She stood there, feeling the delightfully warm air blowing over her neck and into the open front of her jacket.

Gil addressed the question first. Apparently he wasn't shy about organizational matters. "Want me to follow you or ride with you?"

"Will you want the freedom to take off? Because once I get there, I'm going to be there for at least a couple of hours."

"I think that I can manage a couple of hours," he said wryly.

"Then hop in."

The ride out to the Baker ranch required nearly an hour of slogging over bumpy roads. Pavement had begun to buckle as usual when water had seeped into cracks and then froze. Gravel roads hadn't been graded in a while. Miri concentrated on driving and left Gil with his own thoughts. She figured if he wanted conversation he knew how to start one.

It was nice to have her window cracked open during the drive. The ground hadn't really started to thaw, and all the growing things were still locked into their winter naps. But the air was fresh and after a few months of mostly enjoying it for only a few minutes, Miri was glad to indulge more than she'd been able to the last few days.

The Bakers had set up a sign pointing to an elevated area of paddock for parking. Dead grasses were thick, and if the ground started melting it should drain fast enough to ensure no one got stuck in mud. A lot of cars had already arrived, and as Miri parked she got a sudden whiff of barbecue grills heating up and the unmistakable scent of smoking meat.

Betsy had pulled out all the stops. Miri guessed nearly forty people had already arrived. Folding tables groaned under offerings, and a stack of paper plates on one of the tables was held down by a snow globe paperweight. A perfect touch.

Gil helped her carry one container of potato salad, leaning heavily on his cane as he did so. He didn't appear steady on uneven ground yet. Miri grabbed the other, plus the bags of burger buns, and they made their way over to the only empty table left.

Betsy didn't let them get far. Wearing a light jacket, she swooped in, smiling. "I'm so glad you decided to come, Gil. Al always said he was going to bring you out here. I'm just sorry you couldn't get here sooner."

As soon as they had deposited their offerings on the table, Betsy gave Gil a tight hug. He seemed a bit uncomfortable and awkwardly patted her shoulder.

Miri cataloged that for future consideration. Walled off. Totally walled off.

Betsy took Gil with her, introducing him around. Miri smiled faintly and bent her attention toward getting the potato salad ready to serve and putting her buns with others.

Then she wandered over to join her uncle Jack, whose smoker was emitting delicious aromas. "Did you start smoking yesterday?" she asked him.

"How else do you barbecue? You doing all right with Al's friend?"

"Gil's a pleasant guy. Restrained."

"Shut down, most like," Jack answered. "I could see it in Al. Do you remember? It was like every time he came home he'd left another piece of himself behind."

Those weren't the memories of her cousin that Miri was trying to cherish, but she felt her stomach tighten as she acknowledged the truth of what Jack had said. War had been cutting away pieces of Al for years.

Or causing him to lock them away. "Jack? Why do they keep on doing it?"

"What do I look like? A shrink?" He lifted the lid on the huge smoker and began basting the ribs. "Almost done." He said nothing for a few minutes. "I can only answer for Al. He felt a real sense of duty. A need to serve. And, to be brutally honest, maybe a little adrenaline addiction. Anyway, I think Al was always testing himself for some reason. I don't know what his measuring stick was, but he seemed to me to be using one. But all that's my guess, Miri, and it may not apply to Gil at all."

Finished basting that side, he turned the meat with tongs and basted some more. Then he closed the smoker lid. "Not much longer. That's almost to the point of falling off the bone." He stepped back, hanging his tongs on a rack at the end of the smoker, and looked around. "Seems like almost everyone's here. And Gil has found himself a place."

Miri turned to look, too. An interesting place, she thought. The old sheriff, Nate Tate, was sitting in the group, a man who had served in the special forces in Vietnam, followed by thirty years as sheriff here. He'd been retired for nearly a decade now and didn't look a day older. But it wasn't just Nate Tate who made the group interesting. Gil had been found by a phalanx of vets, among them Seth Hardin and a few others who had served in special forces. Even Jess MacGregor, who'd been a combat medic, had joined them.

Edie Hardin, who had her own experiences of combat, had gravitated with her and Seth's child to a group of women. Billy Joe Yuma, formerly a medevac pilot in Vietnam and now director of the county's emergency services, had not joined the group around Gil.

Miri studied the group dynamics and wondered what was going on. The meeting of some kind of elite club, no outsiders welcome? Or something else.

Jack spoke. "Go join 'em."

"I don't belong."

"Exactly." Jack gave her a little nudge. "This is a barbecue to make Betsy happy, not to create a support group."

He had a point. Miri took a couple steps in the direction of the knot of men, then hesitated. There might be a good reason for that huddle. She also suspected there were stories about Al that would never be repeated to Betsy, but that Gil could share with these men of similar backgrounds. Maybe that was cathartic for a man who said very little. Except that he didn't appear to be sharing much. The others were talking, and occasionally a bark of laughter would punctuate the otherwise quiet conversation.

There were other clusters, as well. Nearly sixty people. They'd hardly congregate into one large crowd. Miri had been to lots of large gatherings as a teacher, and crowd breakout was common. Conversation became easier.

Jack was right, however. This barbecue, while ostensibly to welcome Gil back, was really about giving Betsy some happiness again. Not since the funeral had she joined in any social events, but now she had organized one in an amazingly brief span of time. And everyone she had called had evidently arrived to support her and Jack.

Gil was only a small part of it, as Al's best friend.

Betsy had decided to rejoin life. For that alone, Miri would feel eternally grateful to Gil. He'd provided the push she needed, the excuse.

So what did Jack expect her to do? Go break up that huddle of men? She didn't think Betsy would want that, especially since she'd said Gil could just find a comfortable chair and hold court—or not come at all if he didn't want to.

Gil was the excuse. Betsy was the one smiling for the first time in ages, having a bit of a hen party around the folding tables that held enough food for an army. Three other men were working grills with hamburgers, hot dogs and bratwursts.

They were going to need another sixty people to eat all this, Miri thought with amusement. She hoped everyone took home leftovers.

Some folks were eating, some still working on longnecks. Miri decided to go join Betsy and her coterie.

She was welcomed warmly by the women, most of whom she'd known all her life, and returned a tight hug from Betsy. She looked into her aunt's eyes and saw their warm brown depths cloudless for the first time in ages.

"Isn't this fun?" Betsy asked. "And all the more special because we can do it in the middle of winter."

"It *is* awesome," Miri replied. "Thaw or not, I wouldn't have thought of it."

Betsy smiled. "I'm glad I did." She leaned in a bit. "We have to carry on, Miri. You know that. But this is the first time since…then that I've actually felt like doing it." She turned and looked toward Gil and the group of vets. "Most of them were Al's friends, you know. At least when he was home. I'm glad they're talking to Gil."

"You don't want to?"

Betsy looked at her once more. "Later, if you're still around. In a couple of hours the temperature will start dropping again as we head into night, and I think nearly everyone will have left. But Jack was talking about building a fire in the fire pit if you and Gil want to hang around for a little while. Meantime, it looks like Jack is pulling those ribs off the smoker. Want to help?"

Miri helped Betsy carry large platters over to the smoker and Jack began piling half racks of beef ribs on them.

"The aroma," Miri said, closing her eyes and inhaling. "Jack, it smells like heaven."

"So go dig in." Jack winked as she opened her eyes. "I heard the potato salad you brought is great. Same for the coleslaw Betsy made."

It didn't take long for the ribs to disappear onto plastic plates. Ceremony was abandoned as people used their fingers to eat meat that was falling off the bone. Someone had brought Gil a plate laden with meat and potato salad, and he was soon eating with the group around him.

Miri was going to let it go, but it occurred to her that those guys had Gil walled off. Maybe there was a reason for it, but it was possible that others at the gathering might want a few words with him. It wasn't as if nobody knew who he was, or his relationship with Al. Betsy had made sure of that.

So she wandered that way with her ribs and coleslaw, and instead of being cut out, she was welcomed, immediately given a chair while one of the men went to find another.

"You guys having fun?"

"At a barbecue?" Seth Hardin asked. "You better believe it." He cocked his head toward the right. "See my dad? He's practically holding court over there."

"People love him, Seth. They always have."

"Well, not always," Seth replied with a crooked grin. "He says he raised hell in his youth. Anyway, at least Edie could come and bring the youngster with us. I suppose I ought to take my share of responsibility here or Edie will never eat." He nodded toward Gil. "You take care, man. See you before you leave, I hope."

Then Seth beelined toward his father, the old sheriff Nate Tate, and his wife and baby.

Breaking into the exclusive circle had an interesting effect. Some of the vets remained. Others left to go join their wives. Soon other women took the emptied seats and the whole context changed. Conversation began to revolve around local events, and different people took turns clueing Gil in, trying to make him feel a part of the community. He smiled faintly, nodded as he listened and ate, and said very little.

When Betsy joined them, conversation turned to Al and some of his youthful escapades. Laughter accompanied the memories, and Miri took genuine pleasure in watching Betsy laugh. As often as she had played with Al as a young child, she hadn't realized what a scamp he was at times.

"One of the cats climbed up into a tree one time," Betsy recalled. "Now I ask you, how many cat skeletons have you seen in a tree? They tend to find a way to get down as long as there isn't a coyote or something holding them up there. Anyway, Al, all of five years old, was scared the cat would never get down, and it was one he was particularly fond of."

Miri nodded, smiling as she recalled Al with the barn cats. Betsy and Jack got most of them neutered, but kept some so they could breed. Barn cats served a lot of useful purposes out here. Anyway, Al had loved those cats, but there was one in particular, a black cat with a half-white face that he'd almost turned into a house cat.

"It was Benji who went up the tree, right?" she asked.

Betsy smiled at her. "Yup. Anyway, despite me telling him that Benji could find his way down when he was ready, as soon as I wasn't watching Al climbed that tree to get him. The next thing I knew, Al was stuck in the tree with a contented cat sitting on his lap, and no way down."

Laughter passed through the group.

"A tree wouldn't have stopped him once he grew up," Gil remarked.

Everyone fell momentarily silent, then Betsy eased a moment that shouldn't have turned awkward at all. "I have no doubt of that. But at the time I quite enjoyed standing at the bottom of that tree and asking him how much help he'd be now that he was stuck, too."

"Ouch," Maxie Walters said. "Did he get mad at you?"

"No, he just said he'd figure it out. Then Benji jumped down, completely unharmed, and Al was stuck up there by his lonesome. The thing was, without the cat he found it a whole lot easier to get himself down. I had to give him credit for that. He said he'd figure it out, and he did."

"He was like that," Gil remarked. "Always." Then he fell silent again, growing pensive.

He looked so weary, Miri realized suddenly. He evidently wasn't as close to being healed as he'd tried to pretend. It wasn't just the stoicism that she'd seen at the funeral. He looked exhausted.

A lot of the guests were beginning to say their goodbyes, coming to speak to Betsy and thank her. Betsy left their group and began to urge people to take leftovers with them, most especially if they'd brought it in the first place.

Miri heard her aunt's voice on the cooling air. "Please. Where will I put it? No one wants all this to spoil."

"It might freeze tonight," someone joked, but containers of food began to vanish from the tables. Disposable tablecloths and plates quickly disappeared into the ranch's huge trash bin.

"We'll leave soon," Miri assured Gil. "I just want to help with the cleanup. Are you warm enough?"

"I'm fine. Let me know if I can help."

Right now he didn't look capable. She wondered if his ability to recognize his own fatigue had been dulled during all the years of active duty. It wouldn't be surprising. "Sure thing."

She went to help roll up the last of the disposable tablecloths and to fold the tables and carry them into the barn. Jack helped her with an extra-long one. "Gil doesn't look good," he remarked.

"Tired, I think. He mentioned that the docs told him it would take a while to get his energy back. Something about most of it going to healing him right now."

"How badly was he hurt?"

"I honestly don't know. He's not the kind of person who makes you feel that prying would be welcome."

"No," Jack agreed as they leaned the table against the growing stack in the barn. "He also strikes me as the kind of man who must be chafing because right now he can't help. I was thinking."

Miri paused and looked at him.

"Even if he wasn't worn-out, I suspect he wouldn't be too keen to sit around a campfire tonight. Sure, it's a treat for the rest of us, but we haven't spent maybe hundreds of cold nights huddling around one to keep warm."

"I didn't think of that," Miri admitted.

"Just occurred to me. And if I make the offer, he'll

probably feel he has to accept it. Another time. Just get the man home so he can warm up and rest."

She looked over and saw that Gil had risen and was making his way carefully over to Betsy, the uneven ground giving him a bit of trouble. She wondered why he was even out of the hospital. Right now she had the impression he should be in convalescent care. What the hell had happened to him?

"Go get him, Miri. Just drive your car up there and pick him up." Jack was firm. "We'll come by your place to visit him after church tomorrow if he hasn't already moved on."

She turned toward Jack and gave him a huge hug.

"What's that for?"

"You have plenty of reason right now to be hard or bitter. You're not. I admire you."

The light was dimming, but she thought she saw him color a bit.

Then she followed orders, trotting over to her SUV and pulling it up close to Gil and Betsy. It *was* getting colder again. Maybe the thaw was almost over.

She climbed out, feeling the nip afresh, and rounded her vehicle to join Betsy and Gil. "We need to get you home," she said bluntly.

Betsy laughed. "I was just telling Gil the same thing. Dear man, you look worn to the bone. If it's all right, Jack and I will stop by after church in the morning." As Gil nodded, Betsy turned to Miri. "Is that okay by you? I'll pick up some sweet rolls at the bakery like I used to do for Al. Jack will love me forever. He's not allowed to have them anymore, but I think we can make an exception this once."

Leaning very heavily on his cane, Gil said good-bye and eased his way into the SUV. Miri closed the door behind him as soon as he'd pulled his cane inside, waved across the yard to her uncle and gave Betsy a tight hug. "If you need help out here tomorrow, let me know."

Betsy shook her head. "Not much left. Our neighbors did a great job. Now you get that young man home."

Gil had started to feel chilled to the bone, and exhaustion had been annoying him for at least the last hour. He hated his weakness, even though it was temporary, but he'd been taking orders for enough years that following them was automatic. Rest, the doctors said, so he rested. Mostly. Leaving his family behind and driving halfway across the country probably wasn't what they meant by rest.

Nor was this barbecue, not that anyone had given him a chance to do much except sit in a comfortable chair and mostly listen to the conversation. Nobody had seemed to expect him to speak at any length, which was good. What did he have to talk about, anyway?

"I hope you didn't leave early on my account," he said to Miri, feeling a twinge of guilt.

"Absolutely not. Betsy and Jack were thinking about building a fire to sit around tonight, but they were reconsidering. Most of the extended family had already left, too. The air feels like the thaw is almost over."

"It does," he agreed almost absently. Night had begun to settle over the land, early as always at these latitudes this time of year. The hours at the barbecue had showed him a bit of why Al had been so proud of his home. People were friendly, he'd always had food on his plate and a beer in his hand, without even asking. Middle-aged angels swooped by every now and then to replace whatever plate he was holding. Often as not, one of the men who'd gathered with him had brought him another longneck.

They hadn't questioned him, either. No one had wanted to know about his wounds or how they'd happened. Of course, all of them had been in combat and they probably didn't need exact details. But there'd been the lack of pressure of any kind. They'd simply included him in their group and chatted about nearly everything under the sun, mostly things that were happening locally, making him feel welcome and leaving him unpressured.

A pleasant change from the visit with his family in Lansing. It wasn't that he didn't love them, because he did. It wasn't that they didn't love him, he was sure of that. It was that they wanted a different version of Gil York, and after seventeen years in uniform he wasn't about to give it to them. That didn't keep them from pressing him, though. They wanted change. They wanted him home.

And he wasn't at all sure he was anywhere near

ready to go home and stay. Besides, Lansing no longer felt like home. It felt more like a place he visited every year for a week or two. It didn't even qualify as a vacation unless he rented a car and headed for Lake Michigan or the Upper Peninsula.

Years and distance had put a gulf between him and his family, such that he'd felt more comfortable among a group of strangers today. Maybe because they understood where he was coming from.

He suddenly became aware of the silence in the SUV as they made their way back to Miri's house. Silences didn't usually trouble him, but this one did. He was being discourteous.

"Al's friends and family all seem like great people."

"Most of them are," Miri agreed.

A quiet chuckle escaped him. "Only most?"

"There are problematic people everywhere." She laughed. "Some can be enjoyed as characters. Others need to be watched out for. But by and large, I agree with you. Jack and Betsy are great people. So are most of their family. They raised Al, didn't they? And they attract the same kind of people as friends."

Small talk just wasn't his thing. Ordinarily not a problem, but it felt like one right now. He'd spent so much time involved in operations and their executions with a bunch of guys who had a lot of shared experiences to talk about, whether humorously or seriously. Miri was making him aware of a lack in himself. She'd been welcoming, sharing her house with him, feeding him, taking him to the barbecue... Sitting here is stony silence almost seemed like an insult.

"Was it getting colder, or was that just me? I mean, I know the day was fading, I'd expect the temperature to drop, but it was beginning to feel bitter."

"It's dropping," she agreed. "I think our midwinter thaw is over. Anyway, we'll get you warmed up and then you can decide how much is the weather and how much your own fatigue. You can burn an awful lot of energy trying to stay warm." Then she laughed. "I guess you know that. I'll check the weather report when we get home."

When they reached Conard City, he paid attention to the place for the first time. He'd been so tired when he drove in yesterday, he hadn't cared. But now as they drove down the winter-bare streets, he saw compact charm left over from an earlier time. There wasn't much to jar a visitor into remembering time had moved on, apparently leaving this town in its wake.

He tried to focus, but didn't quite make it. He was in a lit-up town again, but the drive home had been a struggle. They'd been far enough out that there'd been no lights to interfere with the star-studded sky.

And for a minute or two, just briefly, he'd been cast back to Afghanistan. He'd managed to cling to the present, but a sour, troubled feeling remained. As did some unaccustomed anxiety.

"Is there some well-lit place where we can get coffee or something?" he asked abruptly. He knew what he needed.

"Sure." Miri didn't even question him. He wondered if she could begin to guess what a relief that was after being at home with his family. He'd been constantly questioned. Understandable, but not comfortable.

"Do you want a bar or a diner?" she asked.

"Diner." He'd been plied with delicious food for hours, but now he was hungry. Really hungry. He'd also been served enough beer that he wasn't sure how many weeks it would be before he wanted to see another. A friendly group, good company, and now somehow he felt as if he'd been through the wringer.

Before he went home with Miri, he needed to be sure he'd silenced the demons that had been awakened by a very dark Wyoming night.

They'd merely whispered to him, but he wanted them firmly shoved down into their pit before they grew louder and possibly disturbed Al's cousin, who'd been so kind to him.

She pulled into a space in front of The City Diner near the center of town. Through the windows he could see a chunky woman at work wiping tables, and only a few other people.

Plenty of space. He needed it.

"Maude's diner," Miri said cheerfully. "Everyone calls it that because Maude has owned it as long as anyone remembers, and she's quite a character. She's even been known to pick your meal for you. I would label her as graceless but not mean. As far as I know, anyway."

He felt miserably stiff as he climbed out of the vehicle and walked into the diner. A lot of things hurt because of his injuries, but other parts seemed to be screaming because of the cold, or maybe years of abusing his body. At this point he couldn't tell anymore. When you let things rest, they had time to stiffen up. Problem was, right now he had to let himself rest, moving only as much as necessary to keep scar tissue loose. He'd failed at that one today.

Inside, the diner was warm. Patched leatherette covered stools, chairs, and benches in the booths. His hip made dealing with a booth problematic, but he chose one anyway, because it would put his back to a wall. The need didn't always trouble him, but tonight it did. Maybe because the drive through the darkness had stirred up some of his PTSD. Sometimes there was just no avoiding it.

He soon saw what Miri had meant about Maude, but she didn't trouble him in the least as she slammed cups on the table along with menus. The coffee was poured quickly, hot and aromatic. It might drive the day's cobwebs away for a bit.

Holding the mug in both his hands, he raised it to his lips and drew a deep breath of the aroma. "Perfect."

"Are you hungry, too?"

"Considering how much food I ate today—all of it delicious, by the way—I probably shouldn't be. I might want a tank topper, anyway."

"Then I suggest Maude's pie, whichever kind she has. She's famous for it."

He managed a faint smile. "It's been a while since I ate pie."

He rested his elbows on the table, holding the hot cup of coffee right in front of his face, watching as tendrils of steam wafted upward, seeing Miri through it. Beautiful woman. Kindly woman. Today he'd had the sense that a lot of people at the barbecue were welcoming him on Al's behalf. A tight-knit community. And the vets who had dominated the group that had gathered around him...

He closed his eyes briefly, feeling it all over again. And he had felt it—men he didn't know, brothers-in-arms, and the brotherhood had come through. They'd surrounded him, trying to make the situation easier for him, as if they understood.

Well, of course they understood. They'd all walked in his shoes and knew that a crowd of strangers could be uncomfortable, at least for a while. The safety net gone, out there all alone, and in many places that had been a threat. It was hard to ease past all that, hence him sitting here with his back to a wall.

He opened his eyes in time to see a large wedge of pie slammed down in front of him. "Dutch apple," said the woman, her tone almost challenging. "What about you, girl?"

"One scoop of vanilla ice cream."

Maude arched a brow. "Reckon you ain't heard it's a cold night."

Miri laughed. "Got me there, Maude. But it sounds good, anyway."

Maude stomped away and Gil looked down at the pie in front of him. "It's warm," he remarked, the scents rising up to join with the coffee he still held. Very warm. He couldn't remember the last time he'd had warm pie.

"A special favor for you," Miri remarked, smiling. Maude returned with her ice cream in a metal dish, then marched away, disappearing into the bowels of the diner behind the counter somewhere.

The last two people in the place got up, threw some bills on the table and headed for the door, nodding as they walked past.

Suddenly the world shook itself back into place, and Gil was able to sip his coffee and dig into the pie. "You were right," he said, after he swallowed the first mouthful. "Best pie ever."

"Be sure to tell Maude." Miri scooped a small amount of ice cream onto the tip of her teaspoon, but paused before she ate it. "What happened, Gil? I could feel something change when we were driving back."

He made it a rule never to open up about most of his experiences to civilians. Yes, something had changed on the drive back, but he wondered what he could recount that wouldn't upset Miri. He'd lived a violent life in service to his country, but he could see no damn good reason to let that violence touch someone like this woman. Yet he sensed he might annoy her, or upset her, if he just shut her out. She was asking sincerely and deserved some kind of answer.

"I don't talk much about my service," he said finally.

"Al never did, either. But after he began to go on missions, when he came home he was different. It was like he knew he was coming from another planet that we couldn't even begin to understand."

"That nailed it," Gil admitted. "Miri, it's a simple fact that I know what I'm capable of in a way most people never will. And it's not something I want to dump all over anyone like you. Someone who's never been there."

She nodded. "I get that. Honestly. Al was frank about it, too. But it seems so sad, like he could never come home again. Like you can't."

Truer than she knew, he thought. But she needed some kind of answer. She'd evidently felt his demons trying to escape during the drive back. He owed her *something*, given the hospitality she had offered so freely.

"It's dark out there at night," he finally said. "You don't find that kind of darkness in a lot of places these days. But you find it in Afghanistan and other places in the Middle East. Jolting down a road in the dark… I guess it stirred some memory or other."

"Does the darkness bother you?"

"Depends." He shrugged one shoulder. "It can be a friend or an enemy. Driving down back roads could be dangerous, though. Sometimes they provided a perfect opportunity for ambush. And headlights didn't always catch the IEDs."

Improvised explosive devices. She knew the term from the news, from Al and from how Al had died. A cold little shiver ran down her spine.

"I vastly preferred to be on foot," Gil added truthfully, then said no more. There was no need to say more. She had her answer, a truthful one even if it was abbreviated. On foot, especially, the darkness was his friend.

But he'd hovered close enough to memory's precipice. Now that he'd told her what had happened, he wanted to change the subject. They were sitting here in a brightly lt diner over coffee and pie. No reason not to enjoy it. "Do you like teaching music?"

"I love it," she said with a smile, a tiny spot of ice cream in the corner of her lips. As if she sensed it, she pulled a fresh paper napkin from the dispenser and dabbed her mouth. Too bad, he thought. He'd have liked to lick it away. And she would have justifiably objected. He enjoyed some internal amusement at his own expense. Here he was, too tired most of the time to do more than sit or pace, with a mangled body, and his genitals wanted to rise to the occasion. Miri was having an unusually strong impact on him. If he'd been capable of carrying out his desires, he'd have been smart to move to the motel.

But he was no threat to her, he assured himself. Al's cousin. A deep bond he still honored, and that extended to respecting Al's family.

Chapter Three

Miri watched him turn his attention to his pie, realizing that the man who had brought Al home really was as reserved and distant as he had seemed that day. He hadn't been controlling his emotions in order to carry out his duty to Al. No. This guy never unleashed any real feeling if he could avoid it. Was he that worried or uncomfortable with his emotions? Did he live behind walls on purpose or by conditioning? She guessed she would never know. Sergeant Gil York had no intention of exposing himself.

"I always loved music," she said, to cover her rather brief response to his question. "I was lucky in that I could play almost any instrument I picked up. Not well enough to claim a position with a band or orchestra or anything, like I said." Then she laughed quietly at herself. "Maybe because I never focused on *one* instrument. Anyway, I was lucky to be good enough to teach it. Although when you have to learn your art as a craft, it makes a difference."

That caught his attention. "How so?"

She tilted her head. "Well, it's one thing to just play from the heart with joy. It's another to break all that down into theory and methods and so on. Teaching makes me be more conscious of the process. Sometimes it can be hard to shake off, enough to just play without ever thinking about it."

He nodded slowly.

"We have a writer in this county, Amanda Laird. She once told me that her writing gets messed up for weeks if people start talking about *how* to do it. She doesn't even like to go to the schools to talk to English classes. And she's death on the idea of themes."

"Meaning?"

Miri flashed another smile. "She says she hates being asked what the theme of her book is. She doesn't consciously plan one, and she gets the biggest kick out of the way her readers participate in the creation by coming away with different reactions and interpretations. So I'm a music teacher and that keeps me out of the clouds, because I have to pass along important basics. What I hope is that my students, after we get past the basics, can use their music to fly again."

One corner of his mouth lifted. "I like that phrasing. I hope they fly again, too."

She dared to ask a question that might turn him once again into granite. "Do you ever get to fly?"

"Only on a troop transport or a helicopter." Then he resumed eating his pie, leaving her feeling like he'd just frozen the conversation.

Then she considered what Gil did for a living. She doubted he could afford to let his head wander in the clouds at all. Ever. His dreams had become a harsh reality, and now there was no room for dreams anymore.

Al had given her the same feeling on his visits. A realist at all times. He hadn't even seemed to want to talk about memories of their childhood, although he occasionally made an effort. *Effort* being the operative word, she thought now.

"Do you guys never think about the future?" she demanded finally.

"Of course. We have to plan ahead."

And that probably said it all. This far and no further. Not five years down the road, but a few weeks down the road. A very narrow telescope for life.

Yet how else could they survive?

She stifled a sigh, spooned the last bit of melting ice cream from her bowl and sipped coffee that was growing cold. That caught her attention immediately. Maude never let coffee get cold.

She looked around and saw that Maude was nowhere in sight. As uneasiness struck her, she said to Gil, "I'll be back in a moment."

Then she ventured into the dragon's lair of the kitchen that served the diner. There she found Maude on the floor, breathing too rapidly, sweat beading her brow. Miri called out instantly. "Gil!"

"Yo?"

"Call 9-1-1 now!"

"I'll be okay," Maude groused, in a voice that was way too weak.

"Sure you will, Maude. But you need someone to look at you. Something's wrong."

But she knew what was wrong as Maude lifted a hand and rubbed the center of her chest.

"Never felt it coming," Maude whispered.

"Women often don't. Just take it easy for now. Soon the medics will be here and you can yell at them."

"Call Mavis. Number by the sink. She's gotta close up."

"Relax. I'll get Mavis. She'll take care of everything. Half the folks in town will probably help take care of everything. You just take it easy until a doc says you're fine."

The call to Mavis was unexpectedly easy. As taciturn as her mother, she said she'd come right away. No histrionics.

Then Miri sat on a recently mopped, still-damp floor and took Maude's hand, watching intently for a change, ready to crawl out of her skin as she waited.

Gil had limped to the doorway and was talking into his cell phone. "Maude at the diner. Yes. She's gray, sweaty and lying on the floor. Still breathing. Conscious."

"Dammit," Maude whispered.

"I agree," Miri answered. She gave Maude's hand a small squeeze. "Hang on. You'll be around to grouse at another generation of customers."

"I'll wait by the front door to wave them through," Gil said. Miri was glad he didn't add that every second counted.

Because it did, and this county wouldn't be the same without the irascible Maude.

It took only six minutes for the paramedics to arrive. Mavis, a younger clone of her mother, wasn't far behind. She took over the task of reassuring Maude, while the medics started an IV and took vitals, talking with someone at the hospital over the radio.

"What can I do to help?" Miri asked as the medics finally wheeled Maude out.

Mavis looked almost lost. She shook herself. "Nothin'," she said. "Mom had most of it done. I just need to take care of the register and lock everything up. Then I can go to the hospital."

"Okay."

"Guess I should put the Closed sign up. Whatever, ain't likely to be serving breakfast by six."

"No." Miri studied Mavis, seeing the near panic in the woman's eyes and the confusion as she tried to absorb everything and make plans. All she wanted to do was follow her mother to the hospital.

"You're sure I can't close up for you?" Miri offered.

Mavis shook her head. "You run on home. I'll do it, won't take long…"

Then she walked to the front door to watch the ambulance pull away, before returning to the back of the diner. "You run home," she said again.

Miri couldn't mistake that Mavis wanted to do this by herself. Maybe needed to do it, just so she'd be busy.

Miri grabbed a receipt book and scribbled her number on it. "You need anything at all, let me know. I mean it."

"Thanks." Mavis looked at the pad, but hardly seemed to see it.

Then there was nothing to do but go home with Gil.

When they arrived at Miri's house, she was surprised to see how early it still was. Well, of course, they'd left the Baker ranch as it started to get dark and cold, which was early at this time of year. Then the long drive into town, stopping at Maude's apparently just after dinner hour, judging by how empty the place was.

So Miri shouldn't have been surprised when she looked at the clock for the first time since morning and realized it was just past eight. Maude would have expected to be open until ten tonight, and to reopen at six in the morning.

Miri didn't know how the woman kept such hours, even now that she had the help of her daughter. But maybe she'd just seen the effects of having no life except work.

She shucked her jacket and flopped on one edge of the couch, leaving it to Gil to decide what he would do. She was disturbed again, but for a very different reason. Now she was thinking about Maude.

"I'm sorry about your friend," Gil said. He'd doffed his parka and now settled with evident caution into the rocking chair.

"She's not my friend. I'm not sure she's anyone's friend, but she sure as heck is an icon in this county."

Gil shifted his weight onto his other side, as if he couldn't quite get comfortable.

"If that chair's not good for you, there's room over here."

He shook his head. "I'm fine. And I'd venture to say Maude must have had a friend at one time. She has a daughter."

Miri couldn't help laughing. "True. And she has two daughters, actually. A few years back, the other one was here for a few months helping at the diner, then she took off. I've no idea where. But there was always a possibility that Maude simply cloned herself."

It was his turn to smile. "Having met Mavis, I'd agree that's a possibility."

Miri closed her eyes a moment, remembering. "Do you think she had a heart attack?"

"I'm not a doctor, but that would be my first guess. It could probably be other things, though."

"If she eats what's on her menu, it's probably the heart. But what a delicious menu. Her steak sandwiches are famous. You need to try one."

Then she heard her own words, implying he'd be around long enough to do that. Hell, she thought sadly, he was probably already on some kind of internal countdown clock, getting ready to move on. Staying in one place for long didn't seem like a quality that being in the Green Berets would nurture.

"Al got antsy when he was home for more than a week or two," she remarked, even though it would sound like a total tangent to him. "He'd help his dad with everything, including livestock, and do a lot of visiting, but even so I could tell he wanted to get back to work. You must be miserable."

"I wouldn't say that." Gil paused as if choosing his words. "After a while the unit becomes your family. Then we have certain ways of doing things that feel orderly to us for the most part. It becomes comfortable. Being away from it is like…"

"Being a stranger in a strange land?"

"Sort of like that, yes. But that doesn't mean I'm miserable. I've traveled through so many cultures in my career that the worst I could say is that this is just another one. We become chameleons. As for Al…" He shrugged slightly. "It's harder to come back to a familiar place."

"Is that what you felt at home in Michigan?"

"Not exactly. My parents moved to Lansing about ten years ago, from Traverse City. It wasn't my childhood home I went back to. I just went back to the same complaints and pressures."

"I guess they aren't getting the message."

"Apparently not." He passed a hand over his face, as if wiping something away. "They'll get their wish soon enough, one way or another. Either I'll be judged unfit to continue on duty, or I'll retire at twenty. Not long now. But I'm not going back to Lansing."

"You don't like it?"

"I'm too old to go back to living near my parents. I can't be their kid again."

"Ah." She thought she got it. Evidently they still wanted him to be the child they remembered, not the man he'd become, and hadn't adapted to his being grown-up. She guessed he hadn't been around long enough for them to get used to the changes. She'd seen it from time to time, when grown children had some difficulty carving out a different relationship with their parents. She would have thought it would be easier for someone who was away as much as Gil.

For that matter, coffee and pie hadn't made Gil look any less weary.

"Gil, you don't have to stay up on my account. If you're tired, go to bed. I'm used to being on my own most evenings."

He nodded, but didn't move for a minute or so. "Thanks for your hospitality," he said at last, then pushed himself to his feet, reaching for his cane. "I'll see you in the morning."

She watched him limp from the room and listened to his uneven gait as he walked down the hall. The man who had marched so firmly and confidently when he'd been here for Al's funeral now walked unevenly and with much less confidence.

God, apart from his injuries and the pain he appeared to still suffer, the changes must be hard to live with. She hoped they were temporary.

She'd forgotten to get her laptop and lesson plans from the bedroom, so she flipped on the TV to some program she hardly watched. Maude. Gil.

A lot to worry about for one day. But she was having a serious problem dealing with finding Maude on the floor like that. The woman had seemed indestructible, as if she'd always be a part of this place. Nothing would be quite the same around here without her. Mavis, though she was a lot like her mother, really wasn't the same.

Swinging around, Miri put her feet up on the couch and leaned back against the padded arm. She felt tired, too. Drained.

She hoped tomorrow would be better. Then she drifted off to sleep.

It was still dark in the morning when she woke. Gil evidently wasn't stirring yet, so she made her way to her own room, took a shower and changed into fresh clothes, a sweater and slacks. In the kitchen she flipped on the radio at a low volume to listen to the weather. Not that she really needed it. The heat was blasting in the house, and there was a chilly draft near the window over the sink. The winter cold had returned overnight. Silently, which seemed strange, but it had come.

She would have expected some wind, she thought as she waited for the coffee and made herself some whole grain toast. A little bluster. Almost as soon as she thought it, she heard the window glass rattle quietly. There it was. Satisfied that her weather sense hadn't flown the coop, Miri stood staring out at the still-dark world while she nibbled her toast, wondering how soon she could call and find out how Maude was doing.

A lot of people would be in for a shock today. Never in the history of the diner had it been closed in the morning. There'd be no coffee, no toast, no scrambled eggs and ham, nothing for the regulars, mostly retired, who camped out there every day, and nothing for the church crowd that occasionally stopped in with their families. The diner wasn't that big, but on Sunday mornings it could groan with all the people.

None of that this morning. Mavis would be tied up at the hospital, most likely, and there was no one else to keep up the flow. Miri hoped Mavis had remembered to call the dishwasher, Maude's only regular employee these days, and tell him he wouldn't be needed.

And all of this was pointless mental buzz, she thought as she took her half-eaten toast and coffee to the table. The diner wasn't her problem. She was concerned about Maude, naturally, but the rest of it… not her concern.

What concerned her was the man sleeping in her office-slash-bedroom, who'd looked almost hollow-eyed last night. As if he were running on his last reserves. She hoped he stayed a few days to catch up with himself before he took to the road again.

But it wasn't just that. Uncomfortable as it made her

feel, she squarely faced the fact that she was attracted to Gil, had been since the funeral and still was even in his beat-up state. She'd been shoving it aside as totally inappropriate and most likely a waste of energy, but the fact remained that she felt seriously drawn to him.

Like she needed that.

At last the weather report emerged from the radio. Not surprisingly, the thaw was indeed over. What she hadn't expected was to hear that the temperature was going to plunge precipitously throughout the morning, reaching below zero around noon. And more snow. While the percentages were far from definite, they faced the possibility of a blizzard later, too.

Great. Well, if Gil had any ideas about hitting the road today, he was going to be disappointed. With sufficient wind, two inches of snow could become a blizzard around here, creating a nearly total white-out. Sensible people would hunker at home, starting this afternoon.

The phone rang and she snatched it quickly. There was an extension in her office that could easily wake Gil.

"Hey, kiddo," said one of her fellow teachers, Ashley Granger McLaren. "Looks like the weather is mad at us again."

"Or decided to return to normal," Miri answered drily. "So what's up?"

"I heard something on the grapevine about Maude. What's going on?"

"I don't know, exactly. She collapsed at the diner

and had to be taken out by ambulance. She was still conscious, though. Beyond that I don't know a thing."

"Well, that's going to upset some applecarts around here. I can think of at least a dozen or more men who are going to *hate* missing their morning at Maude's. Now they'll actually have to stay home with their wives."

Miri laughed. "I hadn't thought of it that way."

"That's because you almost never go over there in the morning before school. I do. I hear it all when I'm buying my coffee. You never heard a bunch of guys with more complaints about everything."

"They're all retired, aren't they? What else are they going to do?"

"Beats me. Well, let me know if you hear anything about Maude."

"Will do." As Miri pivoted to hang up the phone, she saw Gil standing in the doorway of the kitchen. Today he'd donned a sweatshirt with loose slacks. She wondered if restrictive clothing bothered him, because not even for the barbecue had he worn jeans. "Come on in," she said. "*Mi casa es su casa* and all that. How are you this morning?"

"Stiff but fine. Well rested, certainly."

That was debatable, she thought as she took in the dark circles under his eyes. "Grab a seat if you feel like sitting. Coffee?"

"Please."

She went to pour him a mug, speaking over her shoulder as she did so. "I was just debating whether to make breakfast sausage or bacon to go with eggs. Any preference?"

"Either one classifies as manna from heaven."

Smiling, she brought him his coffee. "Come on, they must serve that in the mess hall or whatever they call it these days."

"The hospital didn't believe in fats, and by the time meals reached me they were less than lukewarm. Besides, when I wasn't on base, I was usually dining on prepackaged meals that astronauts wouldn't have envied." He smiled faintly. "On my list of luxuries are hot showers and hot food."

"Well, you're welcome to both here." Reaching into the fridge, she pulled out a roll of breakfast sausage and began to make it into patties. "I haven't heard anything about Maude yet, and I doubt the hospital would tell me a thing if I called. So I guess I have to wait."

"Wouldn't Mavis call you?"

Miri shrugged. "Who knows? She must have much more important things on her mind right now."

"Very likely, unless her mother's been given a clean bill of health."

As soon as she finished cooking the sausage and eggs, Miri put a platter on the table and told him to help himself. He allowed he'd like a few slices of toast, so she made them the easy way, bringing her four-slice toaster to the table and working from there. She didn't much care for cold scrambled eggs herself.

Gil took over making the toast and buttering it for the two of them.

"Do you have someplace of your own to live?" she asked, watching his dexterity with the toast. "Or do you live in barracks or whatever they call it now?"

"I share an apartment with three other men. Most of the time some of us are away, so it never feels crowded. But yeah, I had my own place, sort of. Just didn't make financial sense to get an apartment to live by myself."

"I can see that. Like when I was in college. Three of us shared an apartment. Unfortunately, it didn't always work well."

"But they move on, don't they? Roommates, I mean. A frequent flux."

As he ate, energy seemed to be returning to him, and along with it the attraction she felt. Somehow she needed to get that this was dangerous. Not that she believed he'd be abusive or anything, but Gil was a man used to being on the go, who probably wanted to return to where his unit was stationed, and who might even manage to get himself back into good enough shape that they'd consider putting him in the field again.

Fifteen-plus years of experience had to be invaluable, and she had no idea of the extent of his injuries.

"You know," she remarked, "I always thought it was odd that Al never once had a serious relationship. When we were kids he seemed like the kind of guy who'd eventually want a family."

"Maybe he did. Women certainly fluttered around the guys. But when you have to pack up and go on a moment's notice so often…well, I think that ruined a lot of budding relationships. Which is not to say none of us married and had kids. Just that many of us never encountered that most amazing confluence, a woman who could live with our jobs that we could also want to marry."

Miri smiled faintly. "I don't think that's easy for anyone to find, really. Maybe you guys were just more cautious."

"Meaning?"

"Look at the divorce statistics in the first year of marriage. Seems like most people fly by the seat of their pants."

She was glad to hear him laugh. Maybe the guy was loosening up a bit.

But she doubted he would loosen up much, if ever.

With the kitchen cleaned up and the day growing grayer by the moment, Miri glanced out and saw the trees beginning to toss, bearing their message of a weather change.

"I hope you can stand being cooped up for a while," she said to Gil as she took their coffee into the living room. "Weather's changing, with snow this afternoon and the possibility of a blizzard."

"I thought it was getting colder. Do you think Al's family will still drop in?"

"Probably. There's time for that."

"Good."

Today he skipped the rocking chair for the more upright gooseneck chair. He propped his cane on the arm, the curved handle hooked over it.

"I guess you didn't get to talk with them much yesterday. And they're the whole reason you came out here."

He nodded. "I got to thinking they hadn't seen him in a while before he was killed, and that they might want to know more about how he was, what he was doing...within the limits of operational security, of course. I know I'd have a lot of questions if I hadn't been with him."

"That's thoughtful of you."

"Not really. I think it's what Al would want me to do. The fog of war extends far beyond the battlefield, to the families, who seldom get the straight dope. And I wanted to see you, too, of course."

She blinked. She hadn't expected that. "Whatever for, other than that Al was my cousin?"

Gil shook his head a little. "You stayed with me, Miri. You became part of my memories of Al. And there's another thing."

"Yes?" Her heart sped up a bit as she wondered what was coming.

"I needed to see you differently from the funeral. You were glued in my mind's eye, a young woman so alone, grieving, and playing 'Taps' so bravely. A sad image. So thanks for some more cheerful ones."

Over the months since Al's funeral, Miri's grief had settled down. It never went away, and could still come in waves, but acceptance had arrived. Now, all of a sudden, she felt her eyes prickle with tears she hadn't shed in a while. Forever, she thought. She'd miss Al forever, but in her mind and heart her memories of him would now always be wrapped in the sad strains of "Taps."

"I'm sorry," Gil said swiftly. "I didn't want to make you sad all over again."

She shook her head. "I've never stopped being sad."

"Sorry," he said again. Then he rose and limped out of the living room. She expected him to go down the hall to the bedroom, but instead she heard him grab his jacket and leave through the front door.

He was going to freeze out there, she thought almost absently. Then she let the tears come. Tears for Al. Tears for his best friend. God, life could be so cruel.

Outside, hip notwithstanding, Gil did his best to march along the sidewalk. The wind had grown cutting as a knife, but he was used to it and worse from his time in some cold mountainous countries. He tried to keep his pace even and firm, but his damaged hip still wasn't ready to give him all the mobility he wanted. Of course, the best way to deal with any of this was to push through the pain.

Use it. Loosen up that scar tissue and make damaged joints do their work until he had enough muscle built up to accommodate a full range of motion. At least that was the hope. The docs gave him fifty-fifty at best.

Fifty-fifty was good enough. Gill had faced far worse odds.

He was also beginning to wonder what he was

doing here. Sure, he'd felt he might be able to answer some questions for Al's family. Maybe share a few of the funnier stories they might not have heard. He'd certainly felt it was like an homage.

But there was something else: Miri. He'd never been able to forget her from that day of the funeral. Never been able to forget the way she had stood tall and straight, playing "Taps" for her beloved cousin. That woman had amazing strength.

But over the months they had corresponded, he realized something else was happening. He wanted to see Miri again. Wanted a chance to get to know her. And before his wounding he'd even entertained a few sexual thought about her, although out of respect for Al he hadn't let them go too far. It wasn't that Al hadn't had his share of flings when the opportunity presented, but family was a whole different ballpark.

Miri was a strikingly attractive woman although she didn't seem aware of it. She had a great smile, almost always ready, and a kind demeanor. He imagined that the kids in her music classes thought highly of her.

His mouth twisted a little as he rounded a corner and felt the slash of wind mixed with ice against his cheek. Reaching back, he pulled up his hood. Miri didn't need a personal reference from him, although that seemed to be what he was trying to build. Why?

Pointless exercise. He wouldn't be here long. He had some other people he intended to visit, men and women who'd been wounded and retired for disability, or had just left when their terms of service were completed. People from the history of his own seventeen years in uniform, many of them the kind of friends you could make only when facing danger again and again together.

So today he'd visit with Al's family, then once this snow blew through he'd hit the road again.

And that meant he didn't need to figure out anything about Miri. He might feel attracted to her, but that wouldn't matter. It couldn't matter. He simply would not allow anyone to get that close to him. Not anymore. Al had closed that chapter of his life by dying. It didn't pay to care.

Gil came across a park bench and decided to sit for a few minutes. A pretty park, he thought, despite having been browned completely by winter except for a few evergreens around the edges. It wasn't large, and held only a few playground items. He thought he remembered seeing an even bigger one on his way into town.

Small town, more than one park. Nice. He heard approaching footsteps and looked up to see a face he recognized from yesterday, Nate Tate. The man people had referred to as the old sheriff.

For a retired guy, he didn't look all that old. "Sergeant," Tate said, taking a seat at the other end of the bench. "Getting old has certain requirements, probably not so different from you. Gotta keep in shape somehow, although it's a long way from the old days."

Gil smiled faintly. "Just call me Gil, Sheriff."

"Nate. Ain't the sheriff anymore, but I feel sorry

for Gage Dalton, who is. I retired more than a decade ago and they still call him the new sheriff."

Gil's smile widened a hair. "I'm not surprised."

"Things change slowly around here. Except the weather, which seems to be changing fast today." Nate chuckled. "Good of you to come back to visit with Al Baker's family. I'm sorry I didn't get more of a chance to visit with you yesterday, but it seemed like our younger vets had you pretty well in hand."

"They did." He wondered if Nate was just being neighborly or if he had a larger point to this.

"Vietnam," Nate said. "Multiple tours with the Army Special Forces. I hear you all are branching out wider these days."

"Sometimes," Gil answered cautiously.

"Didn't figure you were going to give me any details." Tate shook his head a bit. "That old French saying 'the more things change the more they stay the same' probably fits. I crossed a lot of borders I prolly shouldn't've crossed, but I had my orders. Anyway, I'm not trying to give you the third degree. You ought to come over sometime. I think you'd enjoy getting to know Seth and Edie better, as well as my daughter, Wendy, and her hubby, Yuma. He was a medevac pilot in Nam. And that Edie's a pistol. She used to fly combat search and rescue. And I guess you know that Seth was a SEAL."

"He mentioned it."

"Well, hang around for a while. You'll find plenty of others in these parts with your kind of background.

And now I need to finish my walk before my wife wonders what happened to me. Take it easy, hear?"

Gil watched Nate Tate stride away, recognizing the easy step of a man who'd walked many miles and knew to keep his knees soft and ready for sudden changes in the terrain. Apparently some things never went away.

Gil rose, too, and started back to Miri's house. He'd heard church bells and decided it wouldn't be long before the Bakers arrived. He didn't want to be rude, although now that he faced the conversation he had no idea what he could tell those people. Their son had shown great courage and had died honorably in the service of his country.

That was the long and short of it. The stuff in between? Most of it no longer mattered or couldn't be shared. A life came down to a single sentence. He supposed a guy was lucky if he got that much.

It occurred to him as he walked the last block to Miri's house that this town was almost trying to wrap itself around him, to welcome him. An odd sensation, but he was having it, quite a contrast to the many towns he'd walked through with the certainty that death might be hiding behind any door.

There was absolutely no reason for this town to give a fig about him one way or the other, good or bad. Maybe he was the one looking for something and projecting it onto the people he'd met. Sure, they'd all been nice, but so what. Common courtesy, was all.

Inside, he doffed his jacket, grateful for the warmth

of the house. Miri popped her head out of the kitchen, asking, "Hot drink?"

"Whatever you've got. It's getting really cold out there."

"I wondered if you'd notice," she said lightly. "Local weather has us down in the single digits now, with more to come. Some reports of sleet."

"I'll second that report," he said as he limped his way to the kitchen. "Felt it sting me on the face once while I was out. Ran into your old sheriff, too."

"Nate? He walks every morning, but usually there's a stop at the diner along the way. I still haven't heard about Maude, by the way."

Gil pulled out a chair at the table. "Surely there's some way to find out?"

"It'll get on the grapevine pretty soon. All it needs is for Mavis to tell one person. Oh, and I'm sorry, but Betsy and Jack won't be coming this morning, after all. Jack was worrying about the weather, and I can't say I blame him. It's a long drive back to the ranch, and just about impossible if there's a whiteout. The wind's already strong—I guess I don't need to tell you that," she said with a little laugh. "Anyway, once snow starts to fall it won't be long."

"I've been in a lot of weather like that. Better safe than sorry." True as that was, he wondered again if he should have come here. Maybe he was rocking a boat and the Bakers were trying to avoid it. Maybe it wasn't just the weather. "Miri?"

"Uh-huh?" She placed a teakettle on the stove and lit the burner.

"Did I make a mistake coming here?"

That seemed to surprise her. She turned from the stove to frown faintly at him. "Why would you think that? Because Jack and Betsy decided they needed to get home before the weather got too bad?"

"Not really."

"I hope not. I haven't seen Betsy this animated since she got the news about Al. She had a truly great week with planning the barbecue. It eased my heart to see how excited and happy she got. So why should you think coming here was a mistake?"

"Because I'm not sure what I'm doing. I thought I'd come and share stories of Al with them, but there isn't a whole lot I can or should share, and there's probably a lot they wouldn't want to hear."

"Then how about you just let them ask questions whenever we get together. There are probably a lot of things they want to know, and I'd bet most of them are very small."

He regarded her steadily. "Small how?"

She shrugged a little. "I'm not a parent, but I some-how don't think I'd want to hear much about my son's war adventures. I'd want to know the little things, like did he often go hungry, did he suffer from the cold… things like that. His comfort. Whether he seemed content with what he was doing. Basically, the one thing he might never talk about with me—did he have re-grets?"

Gil stood abruptly. From time to time he had serious problems being indoors. He felt confined, nearly trapped. "I'm going to step out onto the porch. I won't be long."

"Do you still want that hot drink?" she asked.

"Please," he said over his shoulder, and repeated, "I won't be long."

Because the pain was crawling up and down his side again, burrowing like an auger into his hip. His spine raised a bit of a ruckus, too, reminding him it wasn't perfectly straight anymore, and oh, by the way, did he have *any* idea how much everything else hurt from his continual limping?

Yeah, he knew, and willed his screaming body to silence.

Miri stood chewing her lip while the teakettle behind her began to whistle. Something was going on with Gil, although to be fair she really didn't know him that well. He seemed reserved even now, although she'd wondered if that tower of granite at the funeral had been a man trying to contain a whole lot of pain.

But there was still some of that about him. He hadn't opened up in any really significant way. Maybe self-control of his inner workings was necessary to his survival. Maybe living in a steel tower was a necessity. How would she know?

But watching him now, hearing him wonder if he should have even come to see her family…that seemed somehow sad. And it wasn't because *he* didn't want to talk about Al, as near as she could tell, but because he was concerned he might cause others pain.

Somehow he'd seemed to need to come out here, and now that he was here, he was having second thoughts. Why?

Aw, heck, she didn't know, and had no way to know what was going on inside that steel box.

She turned down the kettle enough to keep it hot without boiling, and opened her pantry to root around inside. Since her aunt and uncle weren't coming by with the promised rolls from the bakery, she had to figure out something for lunch. Since Gil had been out walking in the cold, preferably something warm and filling.

Just about the time she settled on grilled cheese sandwiches with tomato soup, a childhood favorite turned into a comfort food on cold days, the phone rang.

She reached for it, expecting to hear the voice of one of her friends. She almost didn't recognize Mavis, who had never called her before.

"Mom's gonna be okay," Mavis said.

"What happened? Are you all right?"

"I'm fine," she said almost irritably. "It was a heart attack. Not real bad, the doc says, because she got help quick. Thanks."

"I'm just glad I found her. So what's next?"

"She'll be coming home tomorrow, supposed to take a few days off and start a lot of medicines. She don't like that idea, but too bad. Anyway, she wants me to open the diner this afternoon in spite of the weather. Might do short hours until she gets back on her feet."

"I'm sure that's wise. And everyone's going to be so happy to hear that Maude is all right."

"I know I am." Without another word, Mavis disconnected.

Miri took the receiver from her ear and stared at it until she heard the dial tone. Shaking her head, she hung it up on the wall base. Those two women were something else. She supposed she ought to be glad Mavis thought to call her. And it was good news, too.

Wondering if Gil was going to stay outside long enough to turn into an ice sculpture, she opened the fridge and pulled out Havarti cheese for the sandwiches. That cheese was a bit of an extravagance, but sometimes she refused to cut corners. The market had sliced it for her, making it ready to go on sandwiches.

Then she pulled a couple cans of tomato soup out of the cupboard.

This might turn into a very long day.

Gil hadn't pulled on his jacket. Standing outside in nothing but a sweatshirt and camo pants was a fierce punishment as the wind and temperature became more dangerous. It was also stupid.

Like it or not, he'd have to go inside soon, but for now the threat of freezing at least quieted the rest of his body's complaints. Somewhat, anyway.

It had struck him, when Miri had told him that the Bakers wouldn't be able to come over because of the weather, that he really had no idea why he'd come here. Sure, his parents drove him nuts with their constant pressure on him to leave the army. They should have gotten the obvious by now: he wasn't going to quit. He wasn't a quitter. Period. He felt he still had more to offer, although that was up in the air, given his physical state.

But all that aside, he'd come here ostensibly to talk to Al's family about his friend. But what could Gil really share? A few possibly amusing stories. Probably very little that would ease their loss one iota. But he hadn't thought that through clearly, a fact that troubled him.

He wasn't a man given to self-reflection, probably a good thing considering what he did. But now he was reflecting. It had begun just a little after he'd started to recover from his wounds, but he'd pretty much suppressed it. Why? Because it was uncomfortable? What the hell about his life was comfortable?

He sighed and watched the cloud of his breath blow away. His ears were beginning to feel pinched. Time to go in.

The cold had stiffened his hip. He should have kept moving, pacing the porch maybe. Leaning heavily on his cane, he started to take a step toward the door when he was struck by a moment of piercing self-understanding.

He needed more. Al's death had awakened that need in him. Life was too damn short, and his army career might not be enough for him anymore. He wasn't going to quit, no way, but maybe it was time to admit that something was lacking.

Maybe he'd come here to check that out. Unlike him, Al had often mentioned thoughts for the future, had looked forward to returning to work on the family ranch. Gil had never allowed himself to look beyond his eventual retirement. Instead he'd listen to Al spin an occasional dream and tell him he'd make Gil part of it. Not that Gil had ever been sure he wanted to go that way, but maybe Al had been viewing the future for both of them.

Then Gil had had a near-death experience. That might be all that had him unsettled. He could have been killed, and his body had been wrecked. He didn't want to leave the army, but now he had to face what it meant when eventually he'd have to, now or later. He had too much time on his hands to ignore it any longer.

He muttered a curse under his breath and opened the door. Not only had his body been messed up. His brain felt as if it had been put in a blender.

Chapter Four

A couple hours after a truly satisfying lunch, Gil sat in the living room alone. Miri had excused herself to do some work for school. Teachers, she had told him lightly, didn't really get time off.

"What about summer?" he'd asked.

"We get about a month off, from the time we finish closing up our classrooms until the meetings for next year begin. Everything from refresher training to organizing and planning. It's not what most people see from the outside. I work every evening on planning and homework, and fit in at least a few hours every weekend. You should see me in early August, when we start band camp three weeks before classes. I'm running constantly."

Things he had never thought about. Things he'd never had a reason to think about. There was probably a whole lot of that, given the structured, mission-oriented life he'd chosen.

If he were to be honest, perhaps that constant focus he'd developed had been a sort of protection. It wasn't as if he *never* had time to look outside his box. He just hadn't. Didn't.

He stared out the front windows at a world that was steadily going nuts. Just yesterday it had felt like spring. Now the fierce wind was beginning to blow snow around. Snow that hadn't existed twenty-four hours ago.

Much as he suddenly wanted to get in his car and leave, he understood two things: he couldn't drive safely in the approaching weather, and he couldn't leave himself behind. He had become uncomfortable baggage in his own life.

Then there was Miri. He didn't want to be rude to her. She'd opened her house to him, welcoming him almost as family because of Al. Unfortunately, one reason he wanted to leave was because of the sexual heat she awakened in him. It had been a while, but now he was experiencing a virtual storm of hunger inside himself. Even if she felt the same, casual sex would be a lousy way to repay her hospitality.

So far she'd exhibited none of the desire to attract a man that he was used to. No makeup, not that she needed any, hair in that long braid rather than carefully coiffed and clothes that steamed his brain when they clearly weren't intended to: jeans far from skin-tight, loose sweatshirts or flannel shirts, and either socks or boots on her feet.

Everything about her was laid-back and casual. But then, maybe that had something to do with living in this small Western town. He couldn't imagine who would have to dress up around here. Maybe the ranches had been dictating local styles forever.

Then his thoughts flashed back to the funeral, to Miri standing there in a long, dark blue dress, and appearing so small to him, even when she approached to speak to him.

She'd had the strength it took to play "Taps" for her cousin, so he figured her for a very strong woman. "Taps" had a way of bringing people to helpless tears, especially at a funeral for someone they loved. Yet she had stood tall and proud, and not a single note had wavered.

Kudos to her. He'd admired her then, and he admired her now. For example, the quick way she'd responded to Maude. He'd seen the older woman go to the back of the diner and it had never occurred to him there was something wrong. Then suddenly Miri had sprung into action and found Maude in trouble.

Because, according to Miri's explanation later, the coffee was never allowed to cool down at Maude's diner. So Al's cousin was observant and astute. She didn't just brush it aside. She went to see what was going on.

A caring woman, from everything he'd seen, caring and strong. And maybe the nicest thing about her was that she seemed happy with her life.

The phone rang, and she must have answered it in her tiny office space in the corner of the bedroom he was using.

Sitting there, thinking it was time to move again before he began to freeze up, Gil wondered what it would be like to grow up in one town, to know so many people, to have friends you'd known all the way back to childhood.

He couldn't imagine it. His home was his unit. And unfortunately, too many people he had known were gone, some for good. If he had any roots, they were planted squarely in the army...and that was temporary. Never at any point had he viewed it as permanent, simply because every single mission raised a possibility that he wouldn't come back, or would come back as he had this time.

And while he hoped they'd keep him on, even if it meant taking a desk job, he knew damn well that when his convalescence was over they might give him a medical discharge.

Hardly surprising that he was beginning to think about matters he'd held at bay for a long time. He might need to carve out a very different future.

Al's pipe dreams of them working the ranch together had merely been a time-filler for Gil. Something to think about, but something he'd never planned to follow through on. Now it appeared that it might be time to find a plan for himself.

"Hey."

He looked up from his rather gloomy thoughts to see Miri hovering in the doorway. She was smiling.

"Need anything?"

"I'm pretty much okay, except that I'd like to take another walk."

"I don't think that's going to happen right now." She waved toward the window and he realized that while he'd been wandering unfamiliar paths inside his own head, trying to take charge of them, the world outside had disappeared in white. He could barely make out the shape of the house just across the street.

"It looks like a snow globe," he remarked.

"Worse." She entered the room and perched on the edge of the rocker. "We're only supposed to get a few inches, but with the wind blowing this way it might wind up looking like ten feet. You must have seen plenty in Afghanistan and other such places."

He nodded slowly. "Sure. Up in the mountains it wasn't unheard of to get several feet overnight. Of course, that could happen a lot of places when you get into the mountains. I don't need to tell you that."

"Nope. Last I looked, we had some mountains around us," she teased. "But we're in what's called their rain shadow. The dumping usually occurs at higher elevations before it reaches us. Usually. Not always."

He glanced out the windows again. It looked wicked and this had barely started. "But it'll clear out by tomorrow?"

"Maybe not. That phone call I just got was from one of my friends, telling me we're going to have a conference call with school admin this evening. Depending on how it looks, we may cancel school."

"Why decide so early?"

"Because around here, school buses have a very long way to go to reach all the kids. Just as importantly, the plows may not be able to get to many places early enough."

"I hadn't thought about that." But remembering the drive out to the Baker ranch, he figured a school bus would take even longer. "I don't recall Al saying anything about it, not that it's the kind of thing to come up in conversation."

"I doubt it would."

He sensed her studying him in a way that didn't quite go with the casual, pointless conversation they were having. Of course, he wasn't used to this kind of conversation unless it happened over a few beers in a bar with some of his friends. Then they'd get casual, often with humor that might shock outsiders. But inside that circle, humor blew off steam, and it was often black humor.

Then Miri astonished him by asking, "Do you ever let your hair down?"

His gaze jumped to her face. She was serious. "What do you mean?"

"At the funeral, I likened you to granite poured into a uniform. I don't think I've ever seen anyone express so little emotion. I didn't know if that was the real you, or if you were under tight control because of the circumstances. But now you've been here since Friday and I still feel like you're granite. Oh, you've smiled and even laughed from time to time, but it doesn't go deep, does it."

She wasn't really asking, and he felt no real need to explain anything to her. He was what he was, mostly because life had happened to him the way it happened to everyone. You did what you needed to get by... within reason.

But the image she had painted of him caught his attention. Granite? He wasn't sure he liked that. He wondered if he should apologize, although for exactly what, he wasn't certain. But she forestalled him.

"Al was a little like that when he came home, too. There were parts of him well beyond reach. It felt kind of strange to me, because I'd known him so well when we were children. I figured it had to do with experiences none of the rest of us could ever share. But you know what I wondered?"

"What?"

"How many of those parts of him had been left behind on his missions, not just buried but gone for good. Or whether they were still there but had changed."

"My knowledge of Al is limited to the years we served together, Miri. I wouldn't venture to guess how much they changed him." Especially since he'd been going through changes of his own at the same time, and probably pretty much at the same rate, he had no way to measure any of it.

But he wondered what she was hoping to discover. More than one person he'd known in spec ops had noted that when they went home they felt like aliens. No secret in that. Most combat vets probably felt the same way. They'd seen things and done things nobody who hadn't been there could truly comprehend. Best to shut your damn mouth and do your utmost to pretend you'd left all that behind.

"It changes us," he finally said, even though she'd already figured that out. "We don't quite mesh with the rest of the world anymore. Inevitable."

"So you shut down?"

He definitely didn't like this line of questioning. Shut down? He didn't think so. But he was extremely careful about how he spent his emotions. Too big an investment could cost heavily.

Nevertheless, her words struck him even as he argued internally with them. Nothing had been the same since he'd regained consciousness and faced the degree of his injuries, the dawning realization that no amount of recovery would be able to put him back in the field, no matter how hard he tried.

Perhaps the changes had begun even earlier with Al's death, when he'd just put more cement in the chinks in his armor—a temporary patch, it had begun to seem.

But the fact remained that he'd been dealing at some level with the realization that nothing was going to be the same. No amount of denial was going to alter that.

As he looked at Miri, her face so earnest and concerned, he felt obliged to admit something to himself. "I tried to be granite. I guess that made me less than a whole person."

Just saying it caused his mind to teeter on the edge of something deeper and darker. How much of himself had he amputated to do his job? And what would those parts think of him if he brought them back? Being stone had been useful. Being human might give him a whole new set of problems.

Dropping back into civilian life caused a lot of difficulty for many vets. It was never seamless, and sometimes it got crazy and painful. Gil didn't want to be one of them, but he had to admit that as long as he had the job the demons didn't rise very often. No room for them.

That was changing. He'd been fighting it, but he knew that sooner or later he was going to lose. Sooner or later he'd have to find a way to deal with all he'd done and experienced. There was no shame, but there was understanding that he was no longer like people who'd never walked the paths he'd walked.

"It's daunting," he said, though he hadn't meant to. This woman didn't need to hear any of this, nor was he sure he wanted to share it. Outside, even though the light had dimmed a bit with the waning afternoon, he saw the whirling, blinding snow and figured that was probably pretty much what was going on inside him. Or would be going on when he dropped the protective barriers and gave up the denial.

"What's daunting?" she prodded gently when he didn't speak for a while.

"The idea of being a civilian again."

She rose, then surprised him by sitting beside him on the sofa. She surprised him even more by reaching out to lay her hand on his arm. He'd been avoiding human touch for a long time now. It had the potential to slide past his defenses. His skin tightened beneath her hand, tensing at her touch even through his shirtsleeve.

"Why is that daunting?"

"Because the person I've become doesn't fit. Because I've got things locked away I don't want to risk letting escape. Because like everyone else who's ever gone to war, the only place I fit anymore is with others like me."

Rising, slipping away from her touch because it awakened him in ways he couldn't afford, he started to pace. He had to keep moving, keep stretching the scar tissue. After a few turns around the tiny living room, he bent and tried to touch his toes. Better than a couple weeks ago. Looser. But his hip shrieked fit to kill.

"What exactly happened to you?"

The bluntness of Miri's question shouldn't have surprised him. She'd already struck him as a woman who saw the world clearly and had no particular desire to be shielded from its ugly realities. Maybe because she hadn't been exposed to many of them…but then he remembered the story of what had happened to her parents. Ugly realities and she were not strangers.

"I was shot." She didn't need any more details.

"And?"

And she was going to demand them, anyway. He didn't like to talk about it, but even as he considered telling her that, he heard the rudeness in the words he'd speak. She knew what had happened to her cousin. Why not share the latest edition of what happens when you go on a covert mission?

"And?" he repeated. "We were covertly infiltrating a country where we weren't welcome, and we were ambushed. I suppose I shouldn't be alive. I took five bullets and some of the blast from a grenade."

"So you pretty much got chewed up." Her voice didn't waver.

"Sort of. Bullets smashed my hip, injured my spine and managed to miss major arteries. The grenade got me with flash burns and some shrapnel. So here I am."

He hoped she didn't ask more. The edited version was quite enough.

More than enough, it seemed, because walls in his mind were shredding, turning from concrete to flaps of paper blowing in the wind. The memories were not only insistent, they forced their way in, filling his mind's eye with horror and his heart with fury. He was tipping over an edge, and he struggled to catch himself but he couldn't.

In an instant he was back in the place where Al had died. Except Al hadn't died there. They had carried him out after they cleared the threat, carried him and his severed leg and arm for miles to where a rescue chopper could dart in and take him. It had taken the chopper long enough. Long enough for Al to die. Toward the end they might have overdosed him on morphine. Gil couldn't be sure, but Al was in so much agony, begging them to kill him.

The family didn't need to know that, but he couldn't forget it. Would never forget how he had failed his best friend.

But then he slipped again, this time into the place where he had nearly met his own end. Memories of the bullets striking, feeling like a sledgehammer, the explosion and concussion and...

Things began to become muddled and mixed up, turning into a stew of many places, many fights, many losses. They usually got out with everyone alive, but not every time. There were the wounds, the screams, the gore, the memory of people, innocent people, getting caught in a crossfire, memories of the enemy... All of it swirled around inside him, riveting him, taunting him, filling him with anger and pain and grief and hatred and...

He fell into the abyss.

Miri saw Gil freeze and stand as stiff as a statue. Soon, a look on his face, especially his eyes, told her he was no longer with her. He was seeing something only he could see, and it didn't appear pleasant.

A flashback? She didn't know, but wondered. She had some familiarity with them because of her friends but was in no position to say with any surety where Gil's thoughts had gone...or why.

She also didn't know what to do, if anything. Should she try to draw him back to the present or leave him alone?

Leave him alone, she decided. Any sound she made, any movement, could strike him as a threat if his mind had carried him back to war. Better to feel helpless, much as she hated it, than trigger something they both might regret.

Most especially she didn't want to cause him any regret. "Just leave him alone" was a mantra used by some of her friends. It would pass.

So eventually this would pass. Sooner or later, Gil would break free of the prison and return. She just had to be patient and wait.

But she *was* feeling an urgent need to answer the call of nature. She studied where he was standing and where she sat, and tried to envision a trajectory that wouldn't startle him.

Then she heard him expel a huge sigh. After a moment, he moved a bit, as if stiff, and his gaze trailed toward her. "Was I gone long?"

"Not really." A surprisingly short time, considering what she'd heard from her friends. "Five minutes? It must have seemed longer to you. Anyway, if I could run to the bathroom?"

He seemed a little surprised, then frowned darkly. "I'm sorry."

"No need." She rose, trying to appear happy. "Hey, everybody has some problems, right?"

"I don't do this."

She didn't ask what he meant, mainly because she didn't want to stir a pot that might still be simmering. "No worries. I'll be right back and we can talk as much or as little as you want."

Once in her bathroom, Miri was astonished by how much tension had filled her. Hardly surprising considering what an intense man Gil was even when he was trying to be pleasant. There was always an undercurrent to him, a sense that he could spring at any moment. Like a panther or leopard, sunning itself in a tree one second and then grabbing some prey in its jaws the next.

Like a cat, she thought as she leaned against the sink after washing her hands. She'd read that cats never really went to sleep the way people did, that their ears never turned off and they could wake in an instant at a worrisome sound.

Well, in some way Gil was like that. Did he ever really relax? Could he if he wanted to?

Aw, heck, what did it matter? He'd be buzzing out of here as soon as he could.

The main thing was that he was probably feeling pretty uncomfortable right now. He'd said he didn't do that. She could only guess that he meant he didn't flash back to the war. But whatever it was, it had left him exposed for several minutes, and he could be perceiving it as a failure on his part.

So she needed to get back out there and normalize things again, so he didn't get the impression she was trying to avoid him. He didn't deserve that.

Still, the breather had been good. She smiled faintly at her reflection and then marched back to the living room, only to find him staring out at blowing snow, his hands clasped behind his back. Despite having the heat on, she felt a chill snaking through the house. One of these days she was going to have to figure where her weatherizing needed some work.

"I'm thinking about a cup of tea," she said. "You want some?"

He turned a bit, exposing the side of his face. "No, thank you. I'm fine."

It had been a while since lunch, and soon she would need to provide some kind of meal, but Miri found herself drawing a complete blank. Cooking was not at all her favorite thing, though on her own she was quite capable of scrounging up a halfway decent meal from her fridge or pantry.

But now she had someone else to think about. Distracted, aware that Gil was apparently going to share not one thing about what had just happened, she headed for the kitchen. Didn't she have several cans of New England clam chowder? Especially tasty when she threw in some bacon bits, a staple in her refrigerator. They could make anything taste better, from salad to soup to scrambled eggs.

Rearranging cans in the cupboard, she found the clam chowder she remembered, and an unopened bag of oyster crackers. A footstep alerted her and she glanced over her shoulder. Gil had joined her.

"You okay with clam chowder?" she asked. "From a can."

"Haven't had that in ages, and I like it. What can I do?"

"Not much." She smiled. "Canned soup is hard to turn into a group cooking affair." She paused. "Are you all right, Gil?"

"I'm fine," he said immediately. "But I guess I owe you an explanation."

She shook her head as she lifted down three cans of the soup, hoping he would be hungry. "You don't have to explain anything to me. Not a thing."

He took the cans from her hands and placed them on the counter while she brought out the oyster crackers.

"My dad especially loved these crackers with soup," she remarked. "He was a fan of almost every kind of cracker, but these were a treat. I don't know the difference other than shape, but the habit stuck with me."

"I haven't had them in years."

"Well, you can rediscover them this evening. I suspect they didn't get soggy in the soup as fast as a regular soda cracker, because to me they don't taste any different."

"I'll let you know."

When everything was on the counter and she'd closed the pantry, he touched her forearm lightly. "I *do* owe you an explanation, unless you just don't want to hear it. But talking might help me understand what I just did."

At that she gave him her undivided attention. Miri was eager to listen. She felt seriously attracted to him, and that frightened her, because he was a great big unknown.

"I'm listening." Such a lame answer to what she suspected had been a difficult offer for him to make. He'd already pretty much said he didn't talk about anything except to other vets. He felt alienated, different.

Well, he'd been living in a different world from folks like her. Coming back had to make him feel like the odd man out.

She waved him to the table as her teakettle began to whistle. One green tea bag in her mug, boiling water, then she turned the kettle off. Sitting facing him seemed like a safer place than kitty-corner to him. If she grew any more attracted to Gil, she'd be daydreaming about him, wasting her time and setting herself up for a fall. Man, even now he looked scrumptious, but as near as she could tell there was no part of himself that he was prepared to give anyone.

She tamped down her female awareness of him and forced herself to wait patiently. Ordinarily she wasn't short on patience, but Gil had some unusual effects on her. She very much wanted to hear what he might say, and the longer he hesitated the less likely he was to speak.

"I've never had one before," he said slowly, "but I think I had a flashback."

That struck her. "Never?"

His expression grew slightly wry, surprising her. This was a grim subject, she would have thought.

"Never," he repeated. "Not in any real sense. Memories, yes, but not the kind that make me feel I'm right in the middle of it all again. I think I've been too busy. Just about the time something might have begun bubbling up, I was off my leave and back on duty."

"Where flashbacks don't intrude?"

"I can't speak for everyone. For me, no. It was like if I stayed on the rails, I couldn't divert. I diverted today."

When he fell silent in thought, she dared to speak again. "That must be…unsettling, to put it mildly."

"Very," he said bluntly. "I don't like my mind playing tricks on me. It's the best weapon in my arsenal."

She felt her mouth trying to fall open and quickly looked down, lifting her tea bag in and out of the hot water. She liked it strong. "I, um, never thought of my brain as a weapon."

"Of course not. You've never had to. But consider my position. What soldier could function without a brain? A zombie?"

The way he said it drew a small laugh from her. She believed he did so intentionally. Trying to get over rough ground as lightly as possible? "Okay, I get it. It just wasn't a comparison I'm used to drawing."

He nodded. "Anyway…" A sigh escaped him. "That came out of nowhere and I don't like it. Who would? All of a sudden I was back in some of the worst times I've had, reliving them. It's one thing to remember. It's another to relive."

"Absolutely!"

"Maybe I will have some tea. Green tea?"

She nodded. He rose before she could, added some water to the kettle and placed it on the burner. "You wouldn't believe how many places in the world I've drunk green tea. Or some really black tea. Anyway, no point going there, because I can't tell you."

Those last few words seemed to be tied up with a frown that appeared on his face. "I can't really tell you anything," he said after a minute. "I'll just have some tea with you and we'll forget this."

She didn't like the withdrawal. Maybe he couldn't talk about his missions, or even the countries involved, but he could surely share his feelings about it.

"You know, Gil, you not only reminded me of granite when we first met, but now you're reminding me of a bottle of champagne that's been shaken and the top is about to pop."

He lifted his brow at that, and there was not only a change in his expression, but a change in his posture. Not so straight and square, leaning more heavily on his cane… Shrinking? No, not that. Maybe weary, and not just physically.

The teakettle whistled and he ignored it for a few seconds, then seemed to shake himself. "Tea bags?"

"Just sit. I'll get it all. How do you like your tea?"

"Straight. Listen, I'm not helpless."

"I don't think you are. But I'm fussy about people rummaging in my cupboards. Space is limited, so everything has a place."

Another attempt to divert the conversation? she wondered as she pulled out a small canister with green tea bags, plus a mug, and put everything in front of him as he eased into his chair again.

He was soon dipping his own tea bag. "Part of what happened was that I went back to the day Al was killed."

She sucked in a sharp breath. For some reason she hadn't expected that, or to hear it so bluntly. Not with the way he'd been edging around it.

"And to the day I got wounded this last time," he added. "But when it comes to reliving experiences, I'd choose to relive my own wounding a thousand times instead of Al's."

Now she was on unfamiliar ground. She didn't want to sound trite, but what he'd just shared certainly deserved an acknowledgment. "That says a lot," she said carefully. "It must have been horrific."

His jaw worked and his gaze didn't meet hers. He didn't want to talk about it. That was fine by her. She'd learned all she needed to know when they'd been advised not to have an open coffin. Her imagination was already too good.

He dropped his tea bag onto the saucer she'd earlier placed on the table, beside hers. Then he lifted the mug and drank deeply. Evidently his tongue didn't scald easily.

He blew out a long breath. "I've had too much time on my hands," he said, as if that explained it all.

"Too much time for my mind to wander into places it shouldn't go."

She chewed her lip for a moment. "Isn't it going to have to go there eventually?"

"Probably. But I won't complain if it waits a few decades."

He looked at her then, and she was astonished to see a half smile on his face, reflected in his eyes. Talk about a fast mood change.

"I'm not always gloomy and rigid," he said. "I've been known to have a good time and crack a few jokes."

She tilted her head, thinking he was a puzzle. This felt like a non sequitur. "I believe you," she murmured.

"No, you probably don't. No reason you should. When you met me, I had a certain role to perform for my friend and for the army. Now I come here and all you see is someone who's been wounded and isn't even sure he's ready to pick up any thread of life."

That grabbed her attention. "You're just tired," she suggested. "You've been through a lot and you're probably awfully tired most of the time. Wouldn't that be normal?"

"You don't have to make excuses for me," he replied, his smile fading. "I'm not good company. The worst part is that I don't especially care if I am. I came here with some lamebrained notion, thinking I could share a few stories with Al's family that they might enjoy knowing, but I haven't managed it yet. And the main reason I haven't managed it is because all I can damn well think about is him dying!"

Chapter Five

Gil strode out of the kitchen, if you could call it striding while he was leaning on a cane. His hip felt as if fiery pokers were digging into it and that at any moment it might just suddenly give way.

He was glad that Miri didn't follow him, though. He was venturing too near to some things. Flashbacks to those awful hours when Al had been hit, when they'd gathered him up and raced over rugged, defiant terrain to reach the landing zone and the helicopter that might save his life. Six men, using everything training and God had given them to keep up a punishing pace.

But they'd been too late.

Until the day *he* died, Gil was never, ever going to forget Al's screams, his demands and pleas that they just kill him, his prayers that God would take him now. Al had never reached the painless place of shock. He'd never lost consciousness. He'd suffered every damn second.

Until the very end, when he was gone before the chopper set down. Morphine? Maybe. They'd done the best first aid they could, but his wounds were severe, severe enough to have killed him. Maybe the horror was that he'd hung on so long. But then, Gil hadn't seen a whole lot of clean kills in combat. Nope.

He could still hear the sounds, smell the odors, feel the effort, the fear, the bullets blowing out the muzzle of his rifle. He was there again, but without losing his place in time and space. He could still see Miri's living room around him, could hear her stirring in the kitchen. The sound of the wind blowing crystals of snow against the glass reached him. Not a flashback, but a powerful memory.

The memories he could handle. They were never far away. But slipping his cogs and falling into the past? No thanks. Wherever his future might lead him, flashbacks would only complicate everything. Especially if there weren't obvious triggers he could avoid.

He walked over to the wide window that overlooked the street and saw no mercy in the blowing blizzard. Hard to believe that just yesterday afternoon he'd been sitting in the Bakers' ranch yard enjoying the warm sun and a barbecue. Meeting a number of people with backgrounds like his. A welcoming group on a beautiful day.

Now he was looking at winter reclaiming the world, as if it realized it should never have let go. Yesterday had been out of sync, and probably all the sweeter for that.

Out of sync. He rolled the words around in his head, because if there was one thing he'd figured out a long time ago, it was that he was out of sync with the world he was supposed to return to eventually. But now, after being wounded, he felt more out of step than he ever had.

Ah, hell, no point thinking about it. He wasn't a brooder by nature, although since getting out of the hospital and basic rehab, he'd been inclining that way. Probably because he didn't know if the army would take him back in any capacity, let alone special forces. He told himself he could do plenty for his unit without going into the field. There was lots to do, planning missions, setting up schedules… Yeah, he could do a lot of things while leaning on a cane. He could even supervise training.

The question he wasn't prepared to answer was what would he do with himself if they insisted on medical retirement. He couldn't imagine that he owned any skills other than what he'd been doing for nearly eighteen years.

Crap, was he about to become an outdated-model car?

He passed his hand over his face and told himself to cut it out. Of course being wounded had left him pondering a lot of things, everything from mortality to a future.

Remembering Al…well, that didn't help, either. No, Gil never wanted to forget his best buddy, but that loss was so recent and fresh that when combined with the mess of his own body, he was plumbing depths better left to philosophers.

He'd had sixteen years under his belt when he buried Al. Now he was past seventeen and less than a year away from another hash mark for his sleeve. What had he thought? That those hash marks would keep coming indefinitely?

At some point there had to be a reckoning. A time when everything would change. Maybe he hadn't wanted to think about that at eighteen, but now he was thirty-five going on thirty-six, and somewhere in all that time shouldn't he have spent a minute thinking about what he'd do when he mustered out?

Or maybe he'd just believed he wouldn't survive it.

Well, didn't that make him the butt of his own joke.

He started pacing to loosen up, steering his thoughts into happier lanes. He could think about Miri, for example. The more he saw of her, the better he liked her. And the more he wanted to hold her close and explore her subtle curves until he knew them by heart.

It might make him uncomfortable, but that was okay. It was the first time he'd felt a spark of sexual interest since Al's death. At least that part of him was coming back to life.

She was pretty, attractive, sexy as hell when she

moved, even if he suspected she had no idea how she drew a man's thoughts. But he had sensed something else. If he wanted anything to do with Miri, he was going to have to open up more. As long as he kept his distance and tried to remain essentially a stranger, he wasn't going to be her type.

Although did that really matter? She had a life, and he couldn't look at long term when he felt as if he'd been run through a jet engine and come out the other side in a heap of pieces. Everything was screwed up now. Everything. His body, his head, his identity, his future...

Yeah, that guy wasn't going to make it with Miri Baker. She deserved better than that. She deserved not to be hurt.

After a few toe touches and some other stretching, he turned back to the window, watching the world don a new white cloak. It seemed to be in a hurry, as hard as the snow was blowing. Miri's porch railing was drifted over now, and he suspected her front steps were buried, too, though he couldn't see that far through the white cloud.

A true whiteout. He suddenly remembered sitting in the mouth of a cave watching a storm just like this. The whiteout was so great they'd dared to build a small fire farther back inside. Along with the sting of ice that occasionally struck his face when the wind eddied a bit, he'd smelled hot coffee, rations heating. And he'd heard the voices of his buddies.

They were a small group that time, meant to infiltrate without drawing attention. Covered in rags that wouldn't fool anyone for long, up close. One look at their boots would give them away. People in these parts would kill for boots like that, and to see three men wearing them all at the same time? Might as well have worn their uniforms.

But they'd worked hard at staying out of sight, at avoiding villages and shepherds with their flocks. In short, they'd practiced complete stealth.

As he remembered that moment, Gil also remembered why they were there. In and out. Randy was the sniper. Al was his spotter, doing all the complex calculations necessary for the shot.

And neither of them really liked his job. They'd been picked, given an opportunity to bug out if they didn't want to do it. Of course they'd wanted to, before they actually went. How cool was it to be a sniper?

Well, they'd found out. Gil shook his head. He'd been the baggage assigned to watch over them and see that they both got out, if he had to carry them on his shoulders.

They had a job. They did it. And that's as much as they wanted to think about it. Enough that they were necessary.

A lot of his life had been like that, he thought now. Doing what was necessary, leaving as little room as possible to think about it.

Gil heard Miri move almost silently behind him. His senses were still acute.

"Looks like we still have a storm," she remarked.

"Soup's simmering on low heat, so whenever you get hungry we'll eat."

"Thanks. I was just looking outside and remembering a time I sat in a cave watching a storm like this." He turned from the window and summoned a smile. "It's a whole lot more comfortable here."

"I should hope so!" she said with mock indignation.

He offered up a laugh, a sacrifice on the altar of a normalcy he no longer knew. Well, he suddenly thought, this was getting gloomy and maudlin. He had a whole lifetime to sort through his past, and he didn't need to do it this weekend.

He glanced toward the window again. "When is this supposed to be over?"

"During the night. The wind might keep up another day or so, making it impossible to tell that the storm has passed, but…it'll ease, too. I imagine school will be closed tomorrow, though. The radio keeps saying the temperature is falling steadily. We're about fifteen below zero right now, with worse to come, so even if everything clears up and the plows get through, the parameters change."

"How so?"

"Too cold for the kids. What if no one can drive them? What if a bus breaks down? Better safe than sorry."

He got it. And glanced again at the window. "The weather changed fast." As if he hadn't seen it happen before, often to the complete contradiction of the forecast. Life-threatening emergencies could come out of sudden changes like that.

She spoke after a moment or two. "If you're through looking out at the storm, I'd like to close the thermal curtains. The heater is going to be working overtime tonight."

Miri drew heavy-looking damask drapes in navy blue to block out the whirlwind. Almost at once Gil thought he could feel the room grow warmer. A figment of his imagination because he could no longer tell what was going on outside?

He didn't usually fall prey to such fancies, but nothing was usual anymore.

"Gil?"

"Yeah?" He made himself turn toward her, surprisingly difficult when he knew exactly which rut his thoughts were about to fall into. Then she startled him into a whole different rut.

"Are you having survivor guilt over Al?"

He froze. "What makes you think that?"

"I don't know. Something about what you said before you left the kitchen. It wouldn't be surprising, given how close the two of you were."

He felt himself icing over. Some things just weren't meant to be displayed, and that was one of them. All the mixed-up feelings he had about Al's death... What gave her the right to even ask? Because she was Al's cousin?

But then an ugly self-defensiveness surged in him

and snaked past his guard, issuing words he would wish unspoken. "Don't you? Over your parents?"

Her face seemed to shrink. All the energy seeped from her body. "Of course," she said quietly.

He'd attacked and he'd hurt her. He'd thrust a caring question back in her face and awoke feelings that still speared her. That she was probably still dealing with. What was his excuse?

Without a word, he reached for her and, against all his usual rules, tugged her into a tight hug, loosening his hold a bit only when he felt her arms lift and close around his waist.

Then, with his face buried in her sweet-smelling hair, he spoke. Murmured, really. Getting enough air to force the words out had become strangely difficult. His chest ached as if wrapped in a steel belt. Nameless emotions clogged his throat.

"I have lots of survivor guilt," he mumbled. "Al wasn't my only loss. As I rose in rank I took on more responsibility. Every loss fell on my head."

Her arms tightened around his waist, offering silent comfort. At least she didn't offer any trite phrases. His feelings weren't negotiable and couldn't be swept away by anyone else. It was one of the reasons he preferred not to think too closely. This was something he had to live with. Nobody could make it go away.

Nor should it go away. He needed to remember his ghosts, because every one of them counted. They should never be forgotten, not their names, not their faces.

Their sacrifices deserved at least that much. Al was one of many in that respect. Some Gil hadn't known well at all, but they'd still been comrades. And they all remained indelibly imprinted within him.

Only now, holding Miri so close, did his soul recognize how much he had been yearning for human touch. Human comfort. A weakness? Maybe. But he needed it more than he could ever recall. Miri leaned into him, her cheek on his shoulder, her arms snug around his waist, and her very presence in his arms seemed to remind him that he was a human being like any other, and that he was entitled to the good things, not just the bad.

For years now, humor and happiness had been fleeting, as if they had been stolen from more important ventures. He could go to a bar when they were between missions, yuk it up with the others, have a few too many beers and call it fun.

This was different, and this had been missing for a very long time. This went far beyond fun, reaching places within him that had done without sunlight for a very long time.

A woman's embrace. So simple. So profound.

But it was nothing he was entitled to, as his hip hastened to remind him. Shards of steel and glass seemed to penetrate it, and he suspected if he moved wrong his leg would give way. Without even realizing it, when he had reached for Miri, he'd dropped his cane, so if he wasn't careful he'd fall himself. *Damn cane*, he thought, tightening his hold on Miri simply because he didn't want to let go of this precious time. Infinitely precious.

But the pain was intensifying because he wasn't moving, because he'd been standing for so long in one position. There was no way to prevent it from winning. When he needed it, his willpower could be steely, but when it came to his damn hip no amount of willpower could keep it from hurting.

"Miri..." Her name came out a whisper. He loosened his hold a bit.

"Lean on me," she said gently. "Just grab my shoulder. I'll get your cane."

"Are you a mind reader?"

"A people reader," she retorted. "I could feel a tremor. Get yourself balanced."

So he gripped her shoulder and took all his weight on his other leg, which of course was no longer perfect, but for the moment...

Miri bent slowly, as if to give him time to adjust, then as she straightened he felt the head of his cane press into his hand. When she was upright and he was stable, she stepped back, tilting her head and eyeing him. "Why don't you get a walker?"

"Because if I'd had one, I wouldn't have been able to hug you."

He watched the color flare in her cheeks, enjoying it, then the play of a smile around the corners of her mouth. He wondered if her lips were as soft as they appeared. "Good point," she said. "Ready to eat?"

She handled it so easily, avoiding any awkwardness

that might have arisen from his spell of weakness. A remarkable woman. An amazing woman. "Sure," he said, realizing that he *had* grown hungry. "Just give me a few minutes to work out my stiffness."

She pursed her lips. "Are you supposed to get any more physical therapy?"

"Eventually. They want some more healing first and I'm looking at another surgery down the road."

"Well, I guess I can see that," she said. "I'm sure some things can be taxed only so far." She turned. "I'll go set out the soup and crackers."

He watched her walk away and felt a huge heap of loneliness in her wake. Dang. He *never* felt lonely.

Miri didn't know quite how to take what had just happened. The man of granite had reached out to her, obviously seeking some comfort, but how much comfort could she offer? He spoke of survivor guilt about others, as well as Al. And he probably had more problems than that. She couldn't think of a darn thing that could help him.

Who was she, anyway? A music teacher. Training as a teacher and a musician didn't exactly offer a lot of psychological insight. Or any methodology that she'd have felt safe applying to another human being with a major problem. Mostly she was trained to know when she should get a student to the school psychologist.

Good as far as it went. Not good enough to help Gil in any meaningful way. If he even wanted help.

She poured the soup into her grandmother's tureen,

covered it and set it on the table beside the ladle. She skipped the matching soup plates, because it was a cold day and even indoors with the temperature set at an energy-saving sixty-eight degrees, the soup would cool fast enough in deep bowls. Right then she was reaching for warmth.

And Gil. She realized she wanted him to open up to her, and she supposed his revelation would qualify as momentous for him, but for her it was only a tiny peek. Maybe the only peek she'd get into the soul of a totally self-sufficient man.

But as she put out napkins and a bowl of oyster crackers, she wondered if she really wanted to get inside that man's head. Al had considered it important not to talk about where he'd been or what he'd done. When he came home, she'd had the sense that he was wearing a mask the whole time, trying to be the Al everyone remembered, concealing the Al he'd become.

Why should it be any different for Gil? Maybe it really just was as simple as knowing that someone who had never gone where they had could ever begin to understand in any meaningful way. She suspected that much was true.

How much isolation could a person live with? Or flip the question around: How much did she really want to know about what isolated him? Words could skim the surface. Hollywood could romanticize it or glorify it. But the gut understanding?

She shook her head at herself and tried to move past the minutes when they'd held each other. It could never be more than that, a moment of tenuous connection. She would never fully understand where'd he'd been, and maybe he'd never be able to fully come home.

But she knew what had really disturbed her: how she had felt surrounded by Gil's arms. She'd occasionally had boyfriends who hugged her, but nothing had ever felt to her like being in Gil's arms. Everything else in the world had simply vanished. For those few minutes, nothing else had existed beyond her and Gil, wrapped together, while deep inside she had felt herself melting.

Softening. The sensation was amazing. Every bit of tension had fled her body, leaving her warm and soft and in another world. She'd like to feel that again.

It was at that instant that she realized she was undergoing an emotional earthquake. She'd never dreamed that a simple invitation to her cousin's best friend, asking him to stay with her while he was in town, could turn her upside down. Sudden fear gripped her. Fear of herself. What crazy thing was she getting into here? She'd never been a wildly impulsive person, but had chosen to live her life in the calm waters at the edge of life's seas.

Yes, she'd met tragedy. Everyone did. What had happened to her parents had been especially gruesome. Al's death had carved a hole in her. But otherwise she was inclined to be levelheaded and sensible. Unlike some of her friends and acquaintances, she felt no desire to stir life up with drama, either major or minor.

Real drama came along often enough to convince her she didn't need to manufacture any.

Indeed, she avoided it. The loss of Al was still recent enough to sting. To make her ache with the hole he'd left behind. But she could accept that easier than she'd accepted the loss of her parents, probably because Al had been away so much of the time. Little in her life acted as a reminder that a part was missing.

That would all be different for Gil. Al had been a big part of his life for many years now, always there, a part of most everything they ever had to do. Now for Gil there'd be a big hole. And from what he'd said, there was more than one.

She suspected that his wounding had given him too much time to count his dead. That just added an extra agony to everything else he was dealing with. Too much time to think.

At last she heard him coming. She wondered if the cold was affecting him, because his step seemed heavier somehow.

Then he came through the door, nodded at her and eased into the chair he usually used. Miri didn't say anything. While silences in social settings sometimes made her feel chatty, she wasn't inclined to say much right now.

She served him piping hot soup, then offered him the bowl of crackers. When they were both served, she picked up her spoon, raised it to her lips, then paused. This didn't feel right at all.

"Gil?"

He lifted his head. He hadn't started eating. "Yeah?"

"Are you okay?"

One corner of his mouth curved. "Always."

"That's not what I mean and you know it. If I'm getting too personal, just tell me to shut up."

He picked up his spoon, but instead of dipping it in the chowder, he turned it slowly in his hand, as if watching the play of light. Outside, the banshees of winter began to keen, an eerie howling that always disturbed Miri no matter how many times she heard it. Lonely and haunting, occasionally even threatening. It was just the wind, but she invariably had to remind herself of that.

"Are *you* okay?" he asked, turning the question back on her.

"As okay as I can be," she retorted. "Having lost my cousin, having lost my parents… What's the point, Gil? We all suffer losses."

"Exactly," he said as he dipped his spoon at last.

She had no idea if she'd just been shut down or not. She decided to be pushy, a quality she ordinarily avoided but was well aware that she owned. "You have an extraordinary number of them, though."

"Depends on who you're talking to."

God, the guy could be like a lockbox. "I'm talking to you," she finally said bluntly. She scooped more soup into her mouth and felt it scald her tongue. Idiot.

"What are you trying to get at, Miri? Just come out and say it."

"There's more bothering you than pain."

His face darkened, and for a second or two she thought he was going to leave the table and his meal. Not that it was much of a meal.

Then he released a long sigh, like air seeping out of a balloon. "Yeah, I've got a lot of things on my mind. Sorry. I've got to go back for physical therapy and more surgery in a month. Nobody's making any promises. For all I know, this may be the best I get. But I'm also wondering if I'll even have a job after this is over. I'm staring at a big blank where once I had a road to follow. I'm trying not to worry about it too much unless I have to, but it's still hanging out there. I only know how to be one thing, Miri. A soldier. A Green Beret. It's more than a job, it's a damn identity."

Whoa, she thought. She'd gotten her answer and it was huge. His *identity*? But then she wondered why that hadn't occurred to her before. If she lost her teaching job, which was so much a part of her, she didn't know exactly how she'd handle it. But she had an advantage: a townful of people she knew, tons of friends, and every one of them saw her as essential Miri Baker, no matter what she did for a living.

It was different for Gil. Why wouldn't it be? His job was overwhelming, consuming, dangerous…and from what she gathered it didn't leave much room for anything else. It was an entire lifestyle.

She lifted another spoonful of the rich, thick soup to her mouth, but spoke before she ate it. "Have you been trying to think of what else you might want to do?"

"Never had to. Al was always so certain I'd come

back to the ranch with him, and while I didn't think that was the way to go for me, it left the whole question in the distant future. Now the future's here. Take me out of uniform and I don't know who the hell I am."

He shook his head and resumed eating. Taking the conversation as closed, she, too, started sipping her soup again. Well, sipping and chewing. This brand of canned soup didn't short either the potatoes or the clams.

He consumed his entire bowl and she suggested he help himself to more. She wasn't surprised when he filled up again and put a handful of crackers on top. As a big man, a powerful man even now, his appetite seemed natural.

But after eating for a couple more minutes, he spoke again. "I keep telling myself they'll find a place for me. Maybe they will. It won't be in the field, that's for sure, but there's plenty else I can do. Then I wonder if I want to be stuck behind a desk to hand out advice, schedules and discipline. Because that's probably what I'd wind up doing."

"You're a man of action," she suggested.

"Well, I've always been in the action. That much is true. Anyway, in my present condition I'm not much good for anything physical. I'm sure it'll get better with time—"

"But not necessarily less painful," she interrupted.

"No," he said shortly. "No. But I can live with pain. I've been ignoring pain for years. Right now I can't even trust my hip to hold me, but they're going to fix that on the next go-round. That's the hope, anyway."

He insisted on helping with the cleanup despite leaning very heavily on his cane. She didn't protest, understanding the need to help. He wanted more coffee, so she made them half a pot and brought mugs into the living room.

Even with the heavy insulating curtains drawn, she didn't need to look to know the wind was still keening. If she checked her email, she was sure she'd find that school was closed tomorrow. It didn't happen often, but then this kind of weather didn't happen often.

Of course, they didn't often hold a barbecue in January, either. Amused by the contrast between yesterday and today, she sipped her coffee and let Gil enjoy the silence. This situation had to be a bit difficult for him. He didn't know her, yet he was staying with her, and Al didn't provide enough of a bridge between them. Gil might have been more comfortable at the La-Z-Rest Motel, which would at least have given him privacy and the freedom to do as he chose.

Well, she reminded herself, if he needed privacy, he could have gone to the bedroom he was using. She wouldn't have trespassed there short of a house fire, not when he was in there.

He was clearly lost in thought, and from the few things he'd mentioned, she suspected he was wrestling with the idea of an entire life change. Not really a unique situation, but unique to him. It was seldom helpful to remember that others had walked this path.

RACHEL LEE

Each person who walked it had to whack their own trail through the undergrowth.

"I never married," Gil said suddenly.

"Meaning?"

"Just that. Never found time, never made time, never met the right person…who the hell knows."

"Maybe you could do that now." What else could she say?

"Sure. A friend once told me that it was stupid to get married if you weren't already happy with yourself. Right now…well, I hardly recognize myself."

She turned on the sofa, putting her coffee down and facing where he sat on the other end. "You recognize yourself, Sergeant. You're still Gil York. Moving on to a new phase doesn't change that. You learned how to be a Green Beret. It's like we said earlier. If you can learn that, you can learn whatever else you need to know. It may be wrenching for a while, but you can do it." She tilted her head. "From the stories I heard from Al, getting that beret in the first place was pretty wrenching."

Gil closed his eyes for a few seconds before they sprang open, as intense a gray as she'd ever seen them. "You're right. I sound like a whiny baby."

"I didn't say that."

"You didn't have to. Listen to me. Crap, a self-pity party."

"Well, when you're in constant pain and everything's up in the air…"

"That's exactly the time not to indulge." He shook

his head as if to escape an annoying mosquito. "I'm beginning to discover that perhaps I'm not best left alone with my thoughts for too long. I'm used to being busy all the time, making plans for the next step. Not contemplating my navel."

She couldn't help it; a small laugh escaped her. "I wouldn't call it that, Gil. You've got a lot of things to sort out. You're trying to make plans for an unfamiliar future. That's hardly contemplating your navel."

"It is when I don't have any parameters. How can I plan when I still don't know how this will all turn out?"

"Contingency planning."

He gave her a cockeyed smile. "All the answers?"

At once she felt embarrassed. She was treating him flippantly and he didn't deserve that. "Sorry," she said. "I just feel so helpless. Talk away. I'll keep my mouth shut."

"I don't want that." Then he caused her to catch her breath by sliding down the couch until he was right beside her. He slipped his arm around her shoulders, and, despite her surprise, it seemed the most natural thing in the world to lean into him and finally let her head come to rest on his shoulder.

"Holding you is nice," he said quietly. "You quiet the rat race in my head. Does that sound awful?"

How could it? she wondered, when she'd been amazed at the way he had caused her to melt, as if everything else went away and she was in a warm, soft, safe space. If she could offer him any part of that, she would, gladly.

"If that sounds like I'm using you…"

"Man, don't you ever stop? Do you ever just go with the flow?" Turning and tilting her head a bit, she pressed a quick kiss on his lips.

"What the…" He sounded surprised.

"You're analyzing constantly," she told him. "This isn't a mission. Let it go. *Let go.* Just relax and hold me, and I hope you're enjoying it as much as I am."

Because she was. That wonderful melting filled her again, leaving her soft and very, very content. Maybe even happy.

"You are?" he murmured.

"I am. More than I've ever enjoyed a hug." God, had she ever been this blunt with a man before? But this guy was so bound up behind his walls and draw-bridges she wondered if she'd need a sledgehammer to get through.

But then she remembered Al and the distance she'd sensed in him during his visits. Not exactly alone, but alone among family. These guys had been deeply changed by their training and experience. Where did they find comfort now? Real comfort?

Her thoughts were slipping away in response to a growing anticipation and anxiety. She was close, so close to him, and his strength drew her like a bee to nectar. He even smelled good, still carrying the scents from the storm outside and his earlier shower, but beneath that the aroma of male.

Everything inside her became focused on one trembling hope, that he'd take this hug further, that he'd draw her closer and begin to explore her with his hands and mouth.

Her breasts began to ache with a hardening need to be touched. An electric excitement passed through her straight to her center, until it was all she could do to hold still.

Her body was making demands of its own, and she was almost afraid to move for fear of rupturing the moment, canceling the growing, hopeful anticipation of his touch. Drawing a breath became difficult, as if all the air had left the room.

Maybe she moved. Maybe he did. She wasn't certain, but suddenly she was closer, and his mouth had sealed over hers, depriving her of the last of her breath.

Reaching up, she forked her fingers into his short hair, pulling his head closer, for an even deeper kiss. His hands, one after another, settled on her back, rubbing up and down, and impatience began to grow. She wanted those hands elsewhere, on her breasts, between her thighs. A primitive drumbeat ran through her blood, drawing her forward into the unknown.

He released her mouth and she gasped for air, throwing her head back, baring her throat. At last, at last his hand moved to her front, finding her breast, covering it, squeezing gently, and in that moment she hated every layer of fabric she was wearing. She wanted skin on skin, everywhere. Just as she was about to pull herself around, to straddle his lap, he began to pull back.

His mouth left hers. His hand dropped from her breast. No!

"Gil?" She could barely summon a whisper.

"Too soon."

Too soon? Who put a timetable on these things? Anger began to seep into the hole left by desire. She wanted to rail, she felt cheated…and she realized she had no right to feel those things.

Eyes closed, releasing a long breath, she twisted away from him until she slumped against the back of the couch. She had no right to demand he take this further. After all, wasn't she one of the people who taught kids at school that no meant no? Men could say no, too.

Eventually she settled down, letting the fever pitch of emotions slip away. Letting sanity return.

"I'm sorry," he said gruffly.

"You didn't do anything wrong." Truth. *Men can say no, too.*

"You're very attractive," he said. "I've been wanting to do that since I got here."

Which didn't answer anything at all. In fact, it sounded like an attempt to patch up her ego, and maybe that wasn't fair. But nothing about this was fair. An attraction existed. He'd made the moves once she was in his arms. And his entire reluctance might stem from his own sense of being a leaf in the wind just now. Perhaps even some misguided loyalty to Al.

The problem was, if he didn't explain why he'd

pulled back, she'd be left guessing. It wasn't right for her to demand he explain himself. Would she want someone to do that to her if she changed her mind midstream? Heck no. And they hadn't even gotten to midstream.

The wind chose that moment to strengthen, sounding desolate as it rattled windows and made the house creak. Winters here could be long and cold, but this kind of savagery was rare.

Finally, she decided she had to do something. She couldn't just sit here like rejection personified. Not good for either of them. "Want some more coffee? Or maybe I could rustle up a dessert."

"More coffee sounds great right now."

Yeah, it probably did. They'd hardly touched the two mugs she'd brought out here. Maybe there'd be enough left in the pot for him. She didn't want any.

He started to rise, but she pressed his arm. "I'll get it. You pace or stretch or whatever you need."

She needed the escape suddenly. She wanted to be in a separate room, where she could be in control of when she next saw him, not waiting here for his return.

She needed to make more coffee. There was so little in the pot it smelled slightly burned. Clattering loudly to let Gil know what she was doing, Miri sought her center, trying to regain her balance.

The man would be moving on in a few days. She needed to find a way to get through this unscathed.

Chapter Six

Miri went to bed rather early, Gil thought. Eight thirty? He must have worn her out with his pity party today. Or offended her by pulling back before exploration could turn into lovemaking.

He couldn't blame her for wanting to escape. He was about as much fun to be around these days as a compost heap.

Anyway, she'd been kind enough to invite him to stay with her rather than at the motel—he'd heard plenty about that place from Al, who'd sworn Gil would stay with the Bakers when he came to visit—and having a houseguest could be wearing. When this weather cleared, he needed to find some way to show his appreciation.

And all those thoughts, every one of them, were dancing around the immediate issue, the immediate reason she'd probably retreated. He might not let many people inside, but that didn't mean he couldn't read them.

He'd seen the emotions flicker across her face, the disappointment, the short-lived rise of anger, then withdrawal. But there wasn't any possible way to tell her that he just didn't want to hurt her. Not Al's cousin. Not Miri.

Because if he'd tried to tell her that, he was certain she would have argued, and he could easily imagine some of it. She was an adult, capable of making her own decisions. True. She could handle it. And maybe she could. But he didn't want to find out the hard way that she couldn't. At least now she'd have to give it some thought, rather than giving in to an impulse.

An impulse he wished they could have shared. He enjoyed women, and not just sexually. He'd had a few relationships over the years, but none of them had been able to make it over the hump of his sudden disappearances…or they hadn't really suited him as time went by. Regardless, stable relationships outside his unit seemed fungible. He wasn't at all sure he was capable of nurturing one long term.

Maybe there was something wrong with him. There certainly was now. Looking ahead at a big blank, with the only red-letter days being his next surgeries, he'd be wise not to get involved.

On the other hand, Miri called to him as no one

ever had. He was still trying to figure that out. Was it because she was like Al in some way? No, she didn't remind him of Al at all. She was very much her own person.

Gil had only to close his eyes and remember her playing "Taps" at the funeral to know how strong and determined she was. Few family members could have achieved that without breaking up. It had required steady breathing, steady hands, no choking... He'd honestly thought she might not be able to do it, and that he'd be pulling out the prerecorded CD and the battery-operated player.

A special dispensation had been made to use a recording of "Taps." There simply weren't enough people in uniform, whether reservist or active, to play it at all the funerals. A military person was entitled to that honor, but not only were they dealing with the fresh casualties like Al, but they had veterans from past wars, all the way back to the Second World War, and there were many, many of them.

But Miri had insisted on doing the honors, and other vets from around here had joined in to give him full honors, from the rifle salute to carrying the coffin. Gil had been surprised, but then wondered what he had expected. Naturally, people who'd known Al would step up.

The wind was knocking at the windows again. Curious, he flipped the small flat-screen TV on and hunted for a weather station. Soon he learned that this storm wasn't likely to blow out before midday tomorrow. Warnings of deadly cold and wind chills ran along the foot of the screen and popped frequently out of the reporter's mouth. The guy was totally intent on his mission to communicate.

Gil turned the volume down, leaving the TV as a distraction, but his thoughts refused to be distracted. Instead of returning to war, however, they returned to past girlfriends. LeeAnn, for example. He'd been seriously thinking about proposing to her until the day he'd found out that she was a sham.

Well, maybe that was unfair, but she'd put a bright face on a whole lot until the day he was stuffing his duffel once again and she flat-out told him she'd had enough of his disappearing act, enough of not knowing where he was going or for how long, or even where he'd been. She was tired of living with fear, most of all. She wanted a man who'd be home every night, not taking off on forty-eight hours' notice for undisclosed locations. Not one she could never be sure would come home in one piece.

Well, he could sure understand that. He was just glad they hadn't tied the knot and maybe had a kid before she realized she couldn't stand it.

One of his buddies hadn't been very sympathetic. "You need to find yourself an army brat," he'd said. "Someone with realistic expectations."

Maybe so, but Gil had never clicked with one, not for long, anyway. He saw some of the other guys making it just fine in marriages, and after he'd blown a few relationships, he came down to one ultimate conclusion. The problem wasn't the women, the problem was *him*.

He hadn't been exactly certain what he was doing wrong, but he hadn't given it a lot of thought, either. His job was always first on his mind, and everything else seemed a distant second.

Until Miri had described him as resembling granite poured into a uniform.

When she'd spoken those words, he'd immediately put them aside. It was good he'd struck her that way. Serving as the noncommissioned officer in charge of Al's funeral had been one of his most painful responsibilities. He'd needed to be granite, because he had to ensure that everything was properly carried out. His last service for his best friend.

But now he wondered. Was he like that all the time? To some extent, he supposed he was. He'd parked himself inside some very high walls to keep the pain and ugliness out. He simply couldn't afford to let things get to him. Period. It would have interfered with his duty, his responsibilities to his men. He had to stay cool as much as possible. In fact, the only time he didn't was when he could justifiably become enraged. That could be useful.

But if he'd truly become what Miri saw, or if that was all that others saw in him, he could understand why women decamped, or made his life miserable enough that he marched away.

So, he was granite. Maybe even deadened inside for self-protection. Except that lately, without the demands of duty to divert him and keep him in line, he was discovering some painful truths.

The first one was that he evidently felt he was in imminent danger all the time. Other than men in his unit, he must feel that no one had his back. That he was out here alone and at risk. He wasn't inclined to trust anyone.

That by itself was bad. He was home now, as reasonably safe as anyone else walking the streets. Safer than he'd ever been in most of the places he'd gone.

But those walls stood between him and the rest of life. A life he hadn't had much time for until now. Did he want to continue this way?

He could remember Al so clearly, talking frequently on long, isolated nights about the future he envisioned for himself when he retired and returned to the family ranch. It wouldn't have been an easy life, but if Al had wanted easy he'd never have volunteered for special forces. And yet the ranch offered promises that couldn't be kept anywhere else: open spaces and plenty of animals to tend. Even horses.

Al had had a special fondness for horses, and some skill with them, as he'd proved more than once during dangerous missions in the middle of nowhere. He'd sometimes found abandoned horses, usually half out of their minds with terror because of whatever had happened in the area. The men couldn't know what had passed, but the horses had made it clear that fright had been stamped in their hearts.

And Al had soothed them and brought them along

and then mounted them. Once he was sure they'd settled, the guys would take turns riding them, when it was safe. A perk, Al called it.

It was more than a perk. Those horses had pleased them all. Then there had been the goats, wandering wild... Well, Al had gathered them up, taught the men how to herd them and had made them lifelong friends in the next town they approached simply by giving the goats away.

Al should have lived.

The corollary to that was that Gil should have died. He was convinced that he didn't have as much to offer, not by a long shot, as Al had. But it was Al who was gone.

Gil supposed a shrink would have had a field day with that. Survivor guilt to the max.

But when a man who believed he had no future thought of a man who had been looking forward to one, how else was he supposed to feel?

He wasn't sure exactly when he realized he was no longer alone. He'd been standing in the middle of the room, generally facing the TV, trying to avoid sitting because of how fast he could stiffen, when he felt eyes on him.

Turning, he found Miri standing at the entrance to the room. She was covered by a thick, dark blue robe that zipped up the front, with matching slippers on her dainty feet.

"Can't sleep?" he asked. Lame question. She was

standing in front of him nearly an hour after she'd excused herself to go to bed.

"No," she answered. Her tone wasn't sharp, and she didn't sound annoyed. Just maybe a bit lost.

She shook her head a little. "I need some tea. You?"

"Sure." He followed her into the kitchen.

She put the kettle on the flame on her stove, shoved her hands into the slit pockets of her robe and leaned back against the edge of the counter. "Warm milk," she said, evidently following her own train of thought. But she didn't move or explain herself.

Then she said forlornly, "I can't stop thinking about Al. I thought the worst was over finally, but now the grief is back almost as fresh as ever. It hurts!" She pulled a hand out of her pocket and wiped her eyes on her sleeve.

Gil stood there feeling supremely useless. What was he supposed to do? What comfort could he offer? Eventually he murmured, "Me, too." A useless but true statement. "Maybe I'm making it harder on you. Tomorrow—"

"Oh, stop," she begged. "You're not causing this. It's just happening. Are you going to tell me it doesn't happen to you, too?"

He couldn't. It had been happening to him this very evening, with the feeling that he should be in the ground, not Al. "I can't."

"I thought not." Her voice wobbled and then she crossed the small distance between them, walking straight into his embrace. He still was leaning on his cane, and right now he didn't dare let go of it. He wrapped his free arm around her, trying to tell her she was welcome. He wasn't at all sure how else to say it.

Her arms closed around his waist, clearly clinging. "Why?" she asked brokenly. "Why?"

"No comforting answers. There aren't any. You want to know the worst part?"

"What?"

"It's all random. Every damn bit of it. Wrong place, wrong time. Your number's up. However you want to phrase it. And that holds for civilians, too. God knows, plenty of them wind up casualties. I won't even talk about kids who get cancer. Random."

She rested against him, her arms tight around him. After a few minutes he could feel that his shirt was growing damp. She must be weeping, but she didn't make a sound.

Damn it all to hell! He wished he could dry those tears, but he believed she was entitled to shed every single one of them. Al's death had ripped a huge hole in her life, too. A man in his prime had been yanked away from everyone who cared about him.

War did that. Life did that. Crossing a street could do that. Part of what he found so awful about it all was that there was never a good *reason*. Argue all you wanted that Al had chosen a dangerous life, but that didn't change the essential thing: his death had still been random. He alone of the unit had been killed. The worst that had happened to anyone else was a bullet graze.

Or take himself. Gil had survived injuries that should have killed him. Why? There were no answers.

So he held a weeping woman and accepted that there wasn't a thing he could do to make her feel better. Maybe he'd even made it worse by coming here and stirring things up. Al was buried and he wasn't. Why should anyone feel good about that?

The teakettle began to whistle. Miri had reached the point of drooping against Gil, the wave of grief having left her weak. She had to summon what was left of her energy to ease back, mumbling, "Sorry," as she went to start making the tea.

"Just sit down," Gil said almost abruptly. "I think I can make the tea for us."

She didn't argue, instead sagging into her usual kitchen chair, resting her elbows on the table and putting her face in her hands. As the flood of grief began to ebb, she realized she wasn't being fair to Gil. She'd lost a cousin, but he'd lost his best friend. Worse, he'd been there when it happened. She didn't want to imagine the horrors that stalked his dreams.

She listened to him open the cupboard, heard the can strike the table gently, followed by the duller sound of two mugs and saucers. Forcing herself to lift her head, she reached for a napkin from the basket she kept on the far end of the table and began to wipe her face. The tears were drying rapidly, leaving her skin feeling sticky and ready to crack.

Soon they were each making a mug of green tea,

both very focused on the simple action of dunking a bag and then allowing the leaves to steep. Banal. Ordinary stuff. Making a cup of tea.

After the wrenching emotions that had just washed through her, it seemed almost ridiculous, yet contradictorily soothing.

"What about you, Gil?" she asked quietly. "You've said little about your injuries."

"Little enough to say. Shot five times. Bullet near my spine still remains. My hip and pelvis shattered. They're putting it all back together a little at a time, waiting for each new step to heal. I'm short a spleen, but they saved everything else. One more surgery, maybe. I hope that's all. Each one feels like starting from ground zero again."

Her heart squeezed. "The bullet near your spine?"

"They're hemming and hawing about whether they want to try to remove it. Basically, if it stays put, they'll probably leave it alone. If not, they've got to take the chance and yank it."

"Chance?" She didn't like the sound of that. Not one bit. "You could be paralyzed? Is that what you mean?"

"Yeah. That's what I mean. It's a chance. That random thing again. I could be perfectly lucky."

"Seems like you could use some luck." She realized she hadn't given a whole lot of consideration to what he must be facing or experiencing. She knew he'd been wounded, that he was in pain, that he needed to stretch scar tissue, but…he could still become paralyzed? It was like the wounding that would never end.

The thought appalled her. He'd been wounded worse than she imagined, and it had taken her this long to ask about it.

"What else?" she asked, determined to face it all.

"Nothing but scars from being wounded, from burns. I have to work at keeping it all loose, but I told you that."

Burns, too. Her stomach felt as if it were on a fast elevator to the subbasement. He shouldn't be suffering from survivor's guilt. He should be suffering from survivor's envy.

"Hey, I'm pretty much in one piece," he said. "It might look a bit like a puzzle, but everything necessary is still there."

"Will you ever be out of pain?"

"I'm not counting on it." He dropped his tea bag onto the saucer and tasted the brew. "You have to tell me where you get this. I've always liked green tea better than black and this one is really great."

"It's my vice," she admitted. "Special ordered from a place on the West Coast."

"Can you put me in touch?"

"Easily. They're on the web." More banality. It was almost as if they were using it like a rope to pull themselves out of the pit they'd dived into. Talk about the easy things, because the alternative was...what? Hell? Most likely.

"Gil?"

He lifted his head, gray eyes almost flinty, but she didn't feel that was directed at her. "Yeah?"

"Do you have *any* idea about what you might want to do if you can't go back to active duty? Simple things?"

"Like what?" he asked almost sharply. "Making paper dolls? Whittling with my KA-BAR?"

She dropped her gaze instantly as her heart began to tap nervously. What had made her ask such a question? She'd already gathered that he wasn't looking down the road of the future. Not yet. He still faced a whole lot before he would really know what he'd be capable of. "I'm sorry. I must be tired, not thinking clearly."

His voice gentled a bit. "No, I'm sorry. It was a reasonable question. So far, no answers. I guess being caught twixt and tween is trying my temper. I can't be sure I won't be cleared for some kind of duty. If I'm not, that's a whole other can of worms. I don't really feel I can plan yet."

"It hasn't been that long yet, anyway," she said quietly. "My world is so different. I can look ahead and see myself teaching until I retire. I can't imagine not being able to do that." Cautiously, she glanced at him again and found one corner of his mouth tipped upward.

"I hear you," he answered. "I used to see it all laid out ahead of me, too. Funny how plans go awry."

There was a good point in what he said. She nodded. "I guess we all tend to think that everything will go on the way it always has. Then something happens."

"Exactly. Something happens. But we get by because we assume we can predict. Guess not."

"Guess not," she agreed. Al had planned a future at his family's ranch, probably had thought he'd settle down with someone local and raise the next generation of Bakers. Gil hadn't looked that far ahead. As for her…maybe she was living in a fantasy world. Miriam Baker, music teacher, surrounded by a tight-knit group of friends and family. Heck, she'd even stopped dreaming of the white wedding that had seemed so important to her back in high school. She rather liked her life now. If something came along to change it all… well, she wasn't so sure she'd be any quicker than Gil at figuring out a different future.

"Random," she said, repeating the word he'd used a little while ago. "It's all so random, but we keep on making plans. Why?"

"Maybe because we like the illusion of control."

She stared at him. "Illusion? Isn't that an odd choice of word for a guy like you? So much must depend on planning."

"We plan, all right. But there's a saying I really like that kind of encapsulates it. 'Every battle happens in the dark, in the rain, at the corner of four map sections.'"

Map sections? It took her a minute to imagine piecing a big map together and the corners of those four sections meeting…and being difficult to read. Maybe not even a perfect match. "Wow," she said.

"So you plan, and to some extent you're still walking blind." He shrugged one shoulder. "Life is a bunch of contingencies, and no plan survives first contact."

"Why plan, then?"

"Because some of it will always come in useful." His smile widened a bit. "Is it driving you crazy that I'm at loose ends?"

"I'm not so sure you are," she admitted frankly. "We all have to roll with the punches. Like when my dad died. Nobody planned that. Nobody planned my mother following him so soon, either."

Gil's smile faded. "I'm really sorry, Miri. That must have been a terrible time for you."

"It was. It was hell. After Dad was killed, the entire family pitched in to save the crops, but then... well, anyway."

"Did you sell the farm?"

"It was always Baker property. Al probably would have worked it along with a cousin or two until he took over the entire operation."

Gil finished his tea. "So the Bakers have a lot of property?"

"Enough. My dad raised the fodder and the herd was fair-sized. So the family made it through even when times got tough, which happens frequently enough on a ranch."

"And what about you? You aren't a part of the family ranch?"

She almost smiled. "Peripherally. The land has never been split up. In a good year, I may receive a small share of proceeds, but I don't count on it. I'm not doing the work. I don't actually deserve anything, and it was more than enough that my dad was able to send me to college. That's a better start than most people receive."

"You're doing well enough for yourself."

"Exactly." She tilted her head a bit. "You know how you said Al always wanted you to become a part of the operation and you weren't especially interested? That's how I am. If I wanted a part in it, they'd make a place for me. Just like Al would have for you. I just know it isn't my cup of tea. I grew up as part of it, and all I could think about was music. I got what I wanted and that makes me very lucky."

"The family seems close-knit."

"We are. Not many would have made it for over a hundred years without splitting the land or having some squabbles over it. They never did. *We* never did. Which is not to say everyone's perfect."

His smile had returned and she was relieved to see it. Her breakdown had been normal, but she couldn't help being a little embarrassed by it. Al was gone, he'd left a big hole in a lot of hearts, but this man was here and now, and he had some pretty big problems of his own.

Imagine having to live with a bullet near your spine, uncertain if you might become paralyzed. Or having your hip shattered badly enough that one operation couldn't put it all back together. It was mind-boggling.

Gil watched the expressions flit across her face. He liked that he could detect the brief changes in her mood as she thought about matters she didn't mention.

He didn't need to know what exact pathways she followed; it was enough to know how she felt about them.

Then, surprising himself, he rose from the table, grabbed his cane and held out a hand to her. "Come sit with me in the living room. Chairs with hard seats are a kind of torture these days."

"Oh! I didn't know. I should have gotten you a pillow." She looked horrified and he couldn't smother a grin.

"How were you supposed to know? Besides, you have a very comfortable couch in the next room. Coming?"

She smiled, an unclouded expression he was glad to see, and took his hand.

Hers felt so small inside his. Delicate. Fragile. Yet those hands of hers must be powerful, too, to play musical instruments. A different kind of strength.

Once in the living room, he sat at the far end of the couch, up against the arm. It gave him some back support, but also gave her the choice of how close to sit. But he didn't immediately let go of her hand, making it clear he didn't want her to draw away.

She didn't even hesitate before she sat right beside him.

"It felt so good when you hugged me," he said frankly. And it was feeling good again. He didn't know how to describe the sensation, except that she softened against him, almost as if she wanted to melt into him, become part of him. He'd never experienced that with anyone before.

He cleared his throat, deciding that this was one time just holding it all in might be the wrong thing to do. If he were reading her body language correctly... And if he wasn't, he might as well know now, because a part of his body was stiffening and beginning to throb, narrowing the focus of his world to the woman beside him.

Such a rare feeling, this hunger, this hovering on the edge of anticipation and uncertainty. The years hadn't jaded him one bit. This woman was precious, and what he wanted from her equally so.

He cleared his throat again and said bluntly, "I want you."

He felt a slight tension in her.

"I realize..." He tried to continue. Realized what? That he'd only really met her two days ago. That all she knew about him she'd heard through Al, and Gil couldn't imagine what that might be. Not even all their Skyping since Al's funeral had been intimate enough to say he knew her.

But he wanted her. And he was startled when she said, "Don't. Just hush and hold me and..."

That was all the invitation he needed. He started to twist his screaming body so he could embrace her, but she took him by surprise. As soon as she drew her hand from his, she reared up and swung her leg over him, tucking her knee into the narrow space between him and the sofa arm. Straddling him. Inviting him.

Her robe rode up, baring her thighs, creating a warm, dark cave between them. Her womanly scents filled his nostrils, enticing him, and when his gaze lifted from that dark, aromatic crevice, it fixed on the zipper that would completely undo her robe.

Not yet, some hazy thought said. *Savor. Take it easy. Slowly...*

But God, it had been so long for him his body didn't want to wait. It wanted to pillage, plunder, take her for a wild ride she'd never forget.

Her hands settled on his shoulders, and his heavy-lidded gaze rose higher, taking in her face, the way her head was tipped back, her eyes were closed. Her breathing had become rapid, and he could see the rapid pulse beat in her throat. She had given herself over completely.

That amount of trust made his throat tighten in a totally unusual way. It also warned him to be careful. Extremely careful. Not only was she Al's cousin, but she had made herself so vulnerable that Gil ached.

All the self-control he'd been cultivating for years proved to be a sham. He knew he shouldn't do this, but he couldn't stop himself. Miriam Baker was a siren, and he couldn't resist the promise she held out right now.

A long, shaky breath escaped him as he gave in. Reaching up, he pulled down the zipper, ignoring the enticements below. The slider on the teeth sounded loud suddenly, ratcheted up his desire.

He'd hardly dared hope she'd be naked under the robe, but she was. As he pulled the fabric open wider, he saw the globes of her breasts hanging before him like delicious fruit ready for his touch. He slipped his hands inside the fabric and found her slender waist, slowly sliding them upward, feeling every curve and hollow, his mouth going dry with anticipation. At last he reached the underside of those globes and lifted her breasts in his hands, squeezing them, drawing a low moan from her. His thumbs found her nipples and stroked them almost instantly into hardness.

Then his view was blocked as he lowered her head and pressed her mouth to his. He gave her entry, and her tongue darted inside his mouth, tasting of tea, and began to drive him nuts by rubbing against his tongue and brushing lightly against the insides of his cheeks.

His body arched upward instinctively, but he stopped it almost immediately, fearing a swelling of pain in addition to the turgidity of his member, which already ached enough that he wondered if he could wait until Miri was with him.

But as he caressed her nipples and returned her kisses, he felt her begin to rock against him. It was going to be over before they knew it.

He pulled his mouth away, drawing deep gasps of air. "Miri…too fast."

"Hush. We can do this again."

He was eager to accept that plan. Very eager.

"Besides," she whispered in his ear as she began to rock against him again, "I want you completely naked."

Well, that wasn't going to happen right now. No escaping it. His mind whirled with sensations. He throbbed and now it was more than his loins. His entire body was one big drumbeat of passion.

Sliding a hand downward, he found that dark cave between her thighs, that aromatic place he hadn't yet explored. As his fingers touched her, he found her damp, but barely had time to register that as a cry escaped her and she pressed herself so hard against him that his hand was caught between her and his rod.

She might as well have poured gasoline on a fire. He felt surrounded by her, trapped by her, and it fueled his desire into a raging conflagration that threatened to burn him into a cinder.

Helplessly in thrall to the needs they shared, they rocked together like a boat on stormy seas until… until…

He heard her cry out, felt her body stiffen against him. Then he let go, feeling as if he turned himself inside out as he jetted his way to completion.

Chapter Seven

Miri felt as if she'd taken a ride in the center of a whirlwind. Collapsed on Gil, she couldn't move, didn't seem able to quiet her heart enough to fully catch her breath.

His arms closed around her back, holding her close, and time passed before she commanded her thoughts enough to wonder about him. "Did I make you hurt?" She hadn't even thought of that as she'd acted like a wildcat in heat.

"You hurt me so good," he murmured. His fingers tangled in her hair and tipped her head so he could kiss her.

Oh, heavens, was she about to lose her mind again? Cave in to the cravings he awoke in her? Surely it was too soon. At any moment reality would come crashing back in and she'd wonder if she was crazy. Because she'd never acted like this before in her life and she wanted to do it again. Soon.

But he stirred beneath her eventually, and, reluctantly, she tried to sit up. He needed to help her. When had every muscle in her body become spaghetti?

"Join me in a shower?" he asked.

She looked into those stormy gray eyes and drew a sharp breath at how soft they looked now. Like flannel rather than flint or granite. If she could help him to look like that all the time...

"It's a small stall," she said, her voice cracking.

"I think we can manage nicely."

They'd hardly be able to squeeze a sheet of paper between them, but that didn't seem so bad. Smiling at the thought, she slid off his lap, again with his assistance, and managed to get stable on her own two feet. She didn't care that her robe still hung open where it had been unzipped.

What she wanted was to see him naked. She'd been denied that so far, and her insides quickened at the thought. He might be wounded, but she was sure he'd be magnificent anyway. Perfection had never appealed to her.

She walked down the hall and turned into her bedroom to use the bath there. Better than trying to stand in the tub in the other room. Even with the mat she'd put down, it always seemed too slippery. In her shower at least, there'd be walls to lean on if necessary.

She reached in, turning the water on to a moderately hot temperature, then closed the door. As she turned she watched Gil enter the bedroom. He looked around, nodding to himself, then moved to the foot of her bed.

He faced her, a crooked smile on his mouth. "Are you ready?"

"Ready for what?"

He shook his head a bit. "Not pretty. But for my lady's pleasure..."

He dropped his cane on the bed and reached for the buttons of his shirt. She ached to help him with that because it would allow her to touch his skin, but as she took a little step his way, he shook his head.

He needed to do this, she understood. Help would have diminished him right now. Okay. She got it. She shrugged her robe off, letting it fall to the floor.

He shrugged off his shirt and tossed it on the bed. His chest was broad, powerfully muscled despite everything he'd been through. Holding her breath, clenching her hands, she made herself wait even as her very core began to grow heavy and throb again.

His arms looked as if he could lift a grown man in each one. She wondered if he always worked out to that degree or if this was some kind of compensation. But then she caught sight of scars in his side and across his abdomen. She bit her lip, holding back any sound of dismay.

He reached for the button on the loose camo pants he seemed to favor, and they slid off him as if they'd long since become too big.

She bit her lip harder as she saw that his legs were nowhere near as heavily muscled as his upper body. They weren't twigs by any means. Nicely shaped…

Oh, Lord, those were burn scars running down one side of his leg. She could almost see the shadow of flames licking up from below. My God, what had happened to him?

He sat on the bed, working on his boots, finally kicking them aside, followed by his socks. Then he stood again and reached for the waistband of his boxers with his thumbs.

"I need to warn you," he said gruffly. "Lots of scars, not all from surgery."

He'd already showed her enough to rip her heart out, but she managed a nod and waited for the rest of it.

His briefs hit the floor, but she barely saw it. He hadn't been kidding. His hip looked like the creation of a mad doctor. Scars. The scars of an awful lot of stitches. No longer smooth. Flesh was gone, and probably muscle, as well.

She couldn't stand back any longer. Closing the distance between them, she reached out with one hand and began to run her palm over him, from the scars in his side, and down to his hip.

"So much pain," she murmured. "Oh, Gil…"

He stood stiffly, letting her continue her inspection, as if he needed something settled right then.

She wasn't in the least repulsed, if that was what he feared. Instead she felt a kind of awe. This man had survived so much, would survive more. She wasn't sure if she'd have been able to endure what he had... and still did.

She found every scar with her hands, pockmarks she thought must be bullet holes, the sharper lines of surgery, the burn scars down the side of his leg...all of it. And as she went, she dropped kisses on them.

Finally, he said through teeth that sounded as if they were gritted, "Shower."

She straightened, catching sight of his renewed erection, and despite everything she laughed.

"Vixen," he said, a grin reframing his mouth from hard lines to soft ones. Lighting his whole face in a way she hadn't seen before. He still had the capacity for laughter, and that delighted her.

The shower stall was tight, but not too tight. It certainly wasn't too tight for him to lather her in every place he could reach. He spent some extra time on her breasts and between her legs, until she was panting.

Finally, she grabbed the bar of soap from him. "My turn."

He even turned so she could get his back. Nothing hidden. Not one damn thing. Then she pulled down the showerhead on its long hose and began rinsing him. She had no idea how long the hot water would last and she didn't think either of them would enjoy a blast of icy water.

"Oh, I like this," he said, taking the sprayer from her and beginning to rinse her. "I can imagine all kinds of trouble I could get into."

The water was just beginning to cool by the time

they stepped out onto the mat. Miri grabbed a stack of towels from the small linen closet and learned that friction could be amazingly delightful, too.

Then, dried at last, he gathered her close and held her.

"You're wonderful," he murmured. "Perfect. Beautiful. Kind. Amazing."

She wanted to answer his extravagant praise in kind, but he swallowed her words with a kiss, making her melt all over again. He was so sweet, and right now he smelled of soap, and the heat from the shower still radiated off him, filling her senses.

Abruptly, reality returned.

"I need my cane." His voice had suddenly grown tight, and he released her.

Before she could offer to get it, he'd propped himself with his hand on the wall and took the two steps to grab the cane. He carried a towel with him as he limped into the bedroom and laid it on the bed to sit on.

The air felt chillier than usual after he released her. Without a word, she went to her closet and pulled out another robe, this one of thick, green terry cloth. Wrapping it around her and cinching the belt, she went to sit beside him.

His eyes were closed, his jaw clenched. She wondered if she should even touch him. "Are you cold?"

He gave a little shake of his head, and she fell silent, waiting for him to deal with the pain that must have suddenly overwhelmed him. She hoped she hadn't caused it.

A couple minutes later he opened his eyes. "I must have moved wrong. That came out of nowhere."

She hadn't realized how stiffly he'd been sitting until she felt him beginning to relax beside her. "That must have been a doozy."

Another one of his patented half smiles. "Yeah. Sorry. Not very romantic."

She pursed her lips and pretended to ponder. "I don't seem to remember asking for romance or that you be romantic. Not that I have anything against it. I'm just pretty sure I didn't ask for it, so don't apologize." Then she grew serious. "Anything I can do to help?"

"Afraid not. It's easing back to normal levels. I'll be fine in a minute."

Then, like a voice out of the depths, her stomach growled loudly. She clapped her hand to her mouth, unsure whether to giggle or apologize.

Gil laughed. "I think we need to feed you something."

She dropped her hand, allowing her smile to show. "I don't usually do that. I'd have a classroom full of hilarity if I ever did. Are you hungry, too?"

"In my line of work, you quickly learn to never turn down a meal or snack." He pushed himself gingerly to his feet. "Shall we go explore?"

She knew what kind of exploring she'd have *liked* to do just then, but figured it would have to wait. Besides, another stomach growl like that would ruin a mood instantly.

She rose, too, and waited, but he waved her on. "I'll be along in a second."

Reluctant to leave him behind—what in the world was going on with her? She was going only twenty feet—she walked to the kitchen and started sorting through cupboards and the refrigerator. Apparently soup and crackers hadn't been enough for either of them. They needed something more substantial, but, honestly, she wasn't used to shopping for more than herself, and even looking forward to this visit she'd assumed she'd just be able to run to the store if she needed anything more.

Enter one inconvenient blizzard. Well, she thought with a secret smile, maybe not so inconvenient. She glanced at the clock on the microwave and realized it was just past eleven. Hardly late, but too late for cooking a real meal. Not that she had many recipes up her sleeve.

She gave a sigh. Life alone, devotion to teaching, not preparing herself in any way, thinking it was great to spend time with her friends, at most getting together with a few other people to do small concerts for church charity…well, she was amazingly incompetent at small things. Most people who lived alone could cook, couldn't they? But at some point she'd decided she hated to do it, and her diet had become simplified and easy. Boxes and cans stared at her, and in her freezer a package of cubed ham for adding to eggs or…

Hmm. She eyed a box of red beans and rice. She

could add some of the ham to that and make it in about twenty-five minutes in her rice cooker.

Because making her life easy had involved lots of handy little appliances, like a rice cooker, and an egg cooker that always delivered perfect eggs even if she became absentminded over her schoolwork. Automated cooking. Yeah, that was her style.

She heard the uneven steps approaching and readied a smile. Gil came through the door wearing a black T-shirt, a fresh pair of dark boxers, and black socks on his feet.

"Are you warm enough?" she asked, genuinely concerned.

He laughed. "I have more clothes if I want to put them on. And when I look at you, I get hot, anyway."

She felt her cheeks flush. They'd been intimate, but she didn't know if she was ready to be so open about it. Gil evidently didn't have any such qualms. He was grinning at her, a totally cloudless expression, and appeared to be enjoying her blush.

"Um...I'm trying to decide what to make for us. Is it too late for you to want a heavy meal?"

"Three squares got left in my distant past. Like I said, I can eat at any time. My stomach lost all faith in the clock a long time ago."

"Okay then. Unless you don't like red beans and rice..."

"Say no more. That's a favorite of mine."

"Well, it won't be restaurant fancy. Straight out of a box with some ham added."

He leaned on his cane and crossed the few steps between them to touch her arm. "Stop apologizing. I've eaten more freeze-dried meals out of boxes and vacuum packs, and cooked over a small paraffin flame, than you can possibly imagine. I've also been at forward operating bases where we took turns doing the cooking with whatever we had, and I can tell you I didn't run into too many French chefs. Whatever you make will be delicious, okay?"

She nodded and felt her blush deepen a little. What was with her? She didn't usually care about such things. She wasn't much of a cook. So what? Was she falling into a stereotype because she was interested in a man? God help her if that was the case. No Donna Reed in this house.

Not that Gil seemed to expect one.

Letting go of her apprehensions, all of which seemed to be pointless, she pulled the rice cooker out of the lower cabinet. A few minutes later, she had added the rice and water, and cubed ham to make a double batch. If Gil was hungry he'd get enough. If not, it reheated well.

She flicked the switch that turned on the rice cooker, then asked if he wanted something to drink.

"Water. I'd really like some water. Where do I get a glass?"

She pointed and let him get it for himself while she poured herself ginger ale. Sitting at the table, she watched him down two full glasses of water from the tap before he brought another glassful to the table with him.

"Man, you were thirsty," she remarked.

"Guess so." He fell silent, staring at the rice cooker, which had just started to billow steam.

She sat with both hands wrapped around her glass, beginning to feel nervous. Was he regretting their lovemaking? Wondering how to extricate himself just as soon as the storm was over? Oh, man, she hoped he didn't think he'd just made a disastrous mistake.

Because for her it hadn't been a mistake at all. No way. Even if he left tomorrow, she would never regret the experience they'd shared.

Closing her eyes, she tried to cement every moment in her mind, etching it so that she'd never forget that this man had showed her pleasures she'd never dreamed of. How or why, she didn't know. It wasn't as if she'd never had sex before, although not very often. But Gil…he'd touched her in places that felt as if they'd never been touched before. Took her to heights she'd never reached. No, she wasn't ever going to regret this.

Then an errant thought crossed her mind, and suddenly Al was there with her, saying, "Told you so."

She caught her breath as she remembered. All the times he'd talked to her about Gil. How many times he said she should to fly out to visit him when he was stateside so he could introduce the two of them.

How she'd laughed, told him not to be silly, and that if Gil wanted to meet the family he could come to Conard County.

The time his crazy grin had vanished and he'd said, "I was talking about you, not the family."

She'd let it pass, but then there were other times he'd said, "You've got to meet Gil. I think you'd get along like a house on fire."

"Sure," she'd answered, and then forgotten about it. But now she remembered all those times, so many over the years.

I told you so. She heard him as clearly as if he stood beside her.

"Oh, Al," she whispered almost inaudibly. He'd been right. She and Gil got on well. But his point had been what? Why did she feel Al was laughing at her right then?

At that moment she remembered another time, when he'd practically twisted her arm to fly back with him when he returned to his station. "You'll like him, Miri. A whole lot."

"What are you? A matchmaker?" she'd demanded, starting to feel pressured and annoyed.

"No," he'd answered frankly. "I just want nature to have a chance to take its course."

That had been his last visit. She'd shoved all that far from her mind from the instant she'd learned that Gil was bringing Al home. Whatever the point behind Al's teasing all those years, it no longer mattered. And she'd believed that she'd never see Gil as anything but the man who had accompanied her cousin's remains home for the last time. A link too painful to be anything else.

Apparently not. Al had tried to tell her. Exactly what, she couldn't know, but he'd been right about her liking Gil. She liked him a whole lot. And right now a little more than that.

"Miri?"

She opened her eyes reluctantly.

Gil eyed her with concern. "Are you okay?" he asked.

"I'm fine. I just remembered something." And now she remembered the few video calls and all the emails she had exchanged so casually with Gil since the funeral. It had seemed light, friendly, not terribly important except that she had wanted to keep in touch with Al's best friend.

But had it been more? She'd learned a little about him. He'd probably learned a lot more about her. Look at them now. There was no way she could think this was light and casual even if she never saw him again. He'd never struck her as a man to do things lightly or casually, and, as she had discovered tonight, she wasn't able to do it, either.

But that was okay, she assured herself. At least she'd have this fantastic memory.

The rice cooker clicked, startling her. It had moved from steaming to spending the next ten or fifteen minutes getting rid of excess water.

Gil still watched her. His attention wasn't unnerving or too intense, however. She rather got the feeling that he enjoyed looking at her more than looking at the walls. That wasn't hard to believe and it wasn't even particularly flattering. A snort of laughter escaped her.

"What's so funny?"

She smiled. "The way you were looking at me. I figured I was easier on the eyes than the walls, but that wasn't especially flattering. I mean, look at the comparison."

A chuckle escaped him, but he shook his head and reached across the table for her hand. "The *Mona Lisa* wouldn't hold my attention as much as you do."

Her heart skipped, but she stuck out her tongue, anyway. "I don't think she's an especially beautiful woman. Wasn't she a self-portrait of Leonardo as a woman?"

"I don't know about that." But his smile was widening. "Okay then, refuse my compliments. I think you're gorgeous, no comparison."

"Now you're over the top." Rising, she got some bowls from the cupboard and soup spoons from the drawer. "Another few minutes. I wish I had some andouille sausage instead of the ham for this, though."

"The ham will be great. I'd eat it without any meat at all." He reached for the bowls and took them from her hands, setting them on the table. "Tell me about teaching music."

"What about it?"

"Well, I gather you love music or you wouldn't teach it. How is it you can survive all the out-of-tune and missed notes of little kids?"

She laughed. "They're learning. And when you

watch them try so hard to get it right, how can you not love it? They also learn incredibly fast. Playing an instrument has an advantage over a lot of other things they try to learn, too. Music gives them instant feedback. They hear when they hit the wrong note and want to correct it. Tone deafness is extremely rare. Most kids are capable of pitch matching, and they're good at it. Many just need a little training."

"The patience of a saint?"

"Not really. I teach all the grades and work with the band and choir."

"Busy, huh?"

"Very. I have aides to help, but not a lot of free time during the school week, or on weekends when there are home games or competitions. But anyway, back to the learning music thing. I had one young woman in tenth grade who got up with her guitar and sang in a talent contest. Gil, she sounded like an angel, and I asked her why she'd never joined the choir. Her answer? 'I can't sing.'"

"Couldn't she hear herself?"

"It wasn't that. When I could get her for a couple of minutes of conversation, it turned out that she'd been hearing all her life that she couldn't carry a tune. I asked her what she thought had happened to change that."

"And?"

"She said she got a guitar and taught herself to play. In the process of doing that, she gained all the mastery of her voice that had been missing before. And she wound up sounding like an angel."

He nodded slowly. "I never thought of singing as being something that could be learned. But I don't sing much."

"This girl was amazing. She could pick out melodies on the piano or guitar without music, and when it came to listening, she had perfect pitch. But *pitch matching...* That had to be learned. Syncing her voice with the notes she could hear in her head, or around her. She got to be pretty good at it, and she was by no means the exception. Given that learning is part of the process of music, because not everyone is a Mozart, I enjoy what I do even more. I watch kids blossom."

A smile seemed to dance around the corners of his eyes, crinkling them attractively. "I like your passion." Then he winked. "*All* of it."

Pleasure rippled through her. She'd have liked to pursue that right now, but she'd promised something to eat, it was ready now and her stomach again offered a plea, quieter this time.

Time to put red beans and rice into the bowls.

Then maybe later... Ah, yes. She hoped there'd be a later.

The pain in Gil's hip eased enough that he enjoyed the supper she'd made and enjoyed helping her clean up. Then he wanted to enjoy something more.

Carefully, he caught her hand and turned her toward

him. He heard her catch her breath, then saw her face reflecting the same eager hope he felt.

After slipping his arm around her shoulder, he limped with her down the hallway to her bedroom, anticipating the pleasure to come. The passion. Because she elicited a strong, deep passion in him, one that drove away common sense and resistance and reason.

He wanted Miri. Beginning and end of it. If there were to be any regrets, they'd just have to come later.

The only light in her bedroom was a small bedside lamp. It had been burning the first time they had come in here, and she'd never turned it off.

For just a moment, he took in the room, really saw it for the first time, and noted that it was bare of girlie frills. Instead it seemed to reflect her straightforward approach to life. Her strength. The bedspread, rumpled from when she had tried to sleep earlier, was a deep blue plaid that matched some scatter rugs. The furniture looked older, probably from her childhood home. The dresser, plain wood, showed numerous dings. A hand-crocheted doily topped it. A chair in the corner was straight-backed and undecorated. Even the curtains were sensible, matching the spread, looking thick with insulation. No pictures on the walls...

Here, at least, she lived like a monk. The rest of her house showed more personality, maybe because she had her friends come over, but back here—her bedroom and her office, which he was using—she'd wasted no money or real time on either one.

But none of that really mattered. The thoughts

skittered quickly through his mind and were just as quickly dismissed as he dropped his cane and reached for the belt of her robe.

Miri was all that mattered. He felt like a kid about to open a present on Christmas morning...a time and place so far away that he was surprised he could recollect the feeling.

But that was what this woman did to him. As easy as it was to slip her robe off and let it fall to the floor, he still swallowed hard, his heart hammering with renewed excitement. Had he ever wanted anything this much?

She was exquisitely formed, at least to his perception. Gently sloping shoulders, a pulse beating in the hollow of her throat like an invitation. Full but not large breasts, enough to fill his hands with their smooth weight. Narrow waist, but not too narrow. A tummy that wasn't perfectly flat, a sign of her womanliness. Then lower to legs that were strong, and knees... When had he ever noticed a woman's knees before? Dancers would have died for these.

He reached out at last, listening to her rapid, shallow breaths as he traced her loveliness from her throat to her hips, and to the secret place between them.

At last she whispered raggedly, "Gil..."

He lifted his hands to lightly touch her engorged pink nipples, and smiled as he saw a shudder of delight pass through her.

But it seemed that his exploration had gone on too long for her. She reached out, gripping the hem of his

T-shirt and pulling it upward. He raised his arms, aiding her until she pulled it off and tossed it aside.

Then she reached for his boxers, his last claim to modesty, because he knew exactly how engorged he was. Almost out of his mind with desire. As she pulled them down, they caught on his flesh, then fell to his ankles.

She took his breath away by wrapping her hand around his erection and squeezing gently, then stroking lightly.

"So smooth," she whispered. "So big..."

Had she just said that? Fireworks went off in his head as he mumbled, "You keep that up and we'll be done so fast."

A quiet little giggle escaped her, one that conveyed satisfaction and delight. She liked her control over him, and truth be known, he didn't mind it one bit.

Then, hesitantly, she touched the collection of scars and dips in his hip. He held his breath, afraid she would find it repugnant despite her earlier response. He was such a mess now...

But she proved that her earlier actions has been honest as she once again bent to scatter kisses on that severely punished flesh.

The last of his self-control fled. Whatever damage his body had taken, he hadn't lost much of his strength.

Bending, ignoring the screech from his hip, he scooped the woman up and managed to keep his footing as he carried her around to the side of the bed and lowered her to the messy comforter. Then he straightened, hoping the industrial-sized pain that drilled him didn't show on his face.

He pulled the comforter from beneath her, mindful that the room was a bit chilly, and drew it up over her. He hated covering that beauty, but he didn't want her to grow cold and distracted. Although at that moment, she didn't look as if anything could distract her.

He rounded the bed, gritting his teeth, refusing to use his cane at this juncture. It would have poked into this incredible moment like an arrow from the past. No reminders, not unless he couldn't avoid them.

He was a little less than graceful getting into the bed, rolling onto his uninjured side. An instant later all the rest ceased to matter because Miri turned onto her side and reached for him.

Flesh met flesh, igniting an instant conflagration. Skin on skin, the most precious and wonderful sensation in the world. Two bodies coming together to join in a single mission of oneness.

His hands roamed her, soon to be followed by his mouth. She wasn't shy, either, her hands searching and touching, and then her mouth found one of his small nipples and he jerked from the unaccustomed sensation.

Oh, man, him too? he wondered. How had he ever missed this?

The pulsing in his body deepened until it reached every cell inside him. He felt her writhing as if she were with him. Musky scents filled the room, adding to the exquisite minutes.

He cupped her rump to draw her closer. Then he ran his hand down the cleft between her cheeks, and it was like setting off a flare.

Suddenly he was on his back and she straddled him, wide open, his for the taking. She rubbed against him, back and forth, and her eyes opened narrowly, looking down at him, as a smile danced around the edges of her mouth. A wide-open invitation.

Miri felt almost as if she were outside of herself as strong sensations pounded through her blood. Want and need had become the same thing, driving her, pushing her, demanding. Her very center grew so heavy and achy that it cried out for a strong firm touch. Yet his hands kept dancing away, teasing her until she felt she would go out of her mind. She buzzed with sensation, feeling as if she had never been this awake in her entire life.

One moment of sanity touched her. Earlier, before they showered, she'd watched him toss a couple familiar square packets on her night table. She reached for one desperately now, which brought her flat down on his chest.

Oh, it felt so good, so *good* to feel his power beneath her, the heat of his skin, the unmistakable movement of his pelvis, trying to claim her. Surely she didn't need to... Her head aswim, she might have let the moment go.

Except that Gil wouldn't let her. He breathed heavily, his eyes almost closed, but he pushed her up and back just enough. When he opened the packet, she snatched it from him and reserved for herself the pleasure of slipping the protection on him, watching his erection dance at the touches, enjoying the way his entire body jerked.

She couldn't wait any longer. Not one minute. Swept away on a tide of tingling, aching, pounding need, she lifted herself a little and he entered her.

It had been so long that she gasped as she felt her soft tissues stretch, but an instant later it felt so good to be filled by him. As if she'd been yearning for this forever.

Need. Was there anything else?

She felt herself carried upward on a tsunami of irresistible force, turning pleasure into pain and then back to pleasure again. She approached the culmination, half terrified, half desperate, because she knew this time it would be so powerful it hurt.

She could never have imagined such a thing, but as she teetered precariously on the tip of the peak, she feared the fall to come. Then she tumbled, crying out in both pain and delight, feeling as if the sensation rocketed through her entire body like a powerful explosion.

Pinwheels whirled inside her as she collapsed, breathless and replete, as minor explosions of delight still rocked her.

Then Gil joined her, with one mighty thrust that

seemed to claim her all the way to her soul. He froze, rigid, then slowly, with a moan and shudder, relaxed.

Then his arms surrounded her and she drifted away into a new universe.

Chapter Eight

They lay together on their backs under a heap of covers, hands entwined. Bodies had long since cooled off; breathing had resumed a normal rhythm.

But that did nothing to erase the magic, Miri thought. She felt as if she had touched the stars and taken a flight to the farthest reaches of reality. She didn't want anything to interfere, to shatter her charmed state of bliss and wonder.

It couldn't last, but she could cling to it for every possible moment. She wanted this night never to end, though she knew it must.

Beneath her hands, granite had become malleable, but no less powerful. He'd bent until they were one, and made a comfortable place for her in his arms. He'd shared himself in the most intimate way imaginable, yet she felt as if a part of him was unreachable. That part had been there from the moment she'd met him, and Miri suspected it would be there until the end of his days.

But she'd come to accept it. It was as irrevocably part of him as the gray color of his eyes. It no longer made her curious or uncomfortable.

Everyone, she thought mistily, had private places within themselves, including her. Places that needn't be shared or couldn't be shared. In her case it was the death of her parents. The grief that had seared her and clawed at her, then had been put away into some sub-basement of her heart.

She sighed, realizing the treasured moments were beginning to slip away much as she tried to cling. Whether they'd ever be able to recover that magic she didn't know. Nor did she know if she'd ever have the chance.

"You okay?" Gil asked, hearing her sigh.

"I think I'm landing. I really don't want to."

"Me, neither." His hand squeezed hers.

Silence returned, except for the sound of the hostile wind outside. In here, next to Gil, she had found sanctuary from the storms, however brief.

Something was happening deep inside her, but she wasn't sure what. She'd dated like any woman her age; she'd even had longer a relationship that had approached the stage of living together. But she'd never,

ever, felt like this, and she feared this was going to leave with Gil.

He'd been here only a couple days. How could she have reached this point so fast? She smothered another sigh so as not to disturb him, and decided there were just no answers for something.

It wasn't as if he'd been a total stranger when he arrived. Al had spoken of him frequently. They'd been exchanging brief emails since the funeral. And then he'd come here and revealed he was nowhere near the stony man he'd appeared to be at the funeral.

A man like any other, carrying a boatload of pain and probably a whole lot of bad memories he couldn't share but had to live with. Yet he still remained caring and even kind, with her, anyway.

And a helluva lover.

A giggle escaped her then, and she rolled over, laying her hand on his powerful chest.

"What?" he asked.

"I was just thinking that you're a helluva lover."

A snort of laughter escaped him. "Wait till my hip gets fixed. I have tricks I haven't showed you."

She liked the sound of that and rested her head on his shoulder, liking the feel of his skin, of his warmth, and the sound of his beating heart. She tried not to take his words as a promise of any kind of future. He'd go back, get fixed up as much as they could, and then he'd have the rest of his life to deal with. Maybe he'd keep his career, maybe he'd have to find something else, but she didn't see how she could be any part of that.

Small-town schoolteacher, with roots as deep around here as any. Wanderlust had never captivated her.

Stop thinking of these things, she advised herself. *Just enjoy the now however long it lasts.*

He covered her hand on his chest with his much bigger one, and she could feel how hard his palms were, hardened from tough use. Not a musician's hands, or a teacher's.

"Do you rock climb?" she asked.

"I can when necessary."

She bet he could do a lot of things when it was necessary. "I thought about it, but got talked out of it. I need my hands for my music. Of course, I need other parts of me, as well."

Another quiet laugh escaped him. "Very nice parts, I might point out. I'd hate for you to lose any of them."

She smiled against his shoulder. "Would you ever rock climb for fun?"

"Conquering El Capitan isn't necessary to prove my manhood."

That caught her attention. An interesting way to put it. Had he left all those things behind? But what would he have left to prove, given all that he must have done? A man without insecurities, at least about his masculinity. She liked that. Some men got past all that, but she had often sensed that in the right situation many guys still thought they needed to prove how tough they were.

How nice to be free of that, although she probably didn't want to know the price he'd paid to get there.

"What else have you avoided because of your music?"

"Not much, I don't think. It's just that at an early age my tutor impressed on me how important it was to take care of my hands. Since then a handful of people have reminded me."

"They're very nice hands," he remarked, stroking the back of the one that rested on his chest. His fingertips caressed her lightly, sending delighted shivers through her all over again. "They charm me when they touch me."

His thoughts ran so close to her earlier ones that she was a bit surprised. Had they developed some kind of psychic link?

"You're gonna hate me," he said, humor in his tone.

"Why?" Her heart skipped an uncomfortable beat.

"I'm hungry again."

She had to laugh. "I think I am, too." Reluctantly, she eased away from him. "Want to eat in bed?"

"Not really. I've got better plans for this bed, and crumbs could be a problem."

He hated to pull on any clothes, but the house felt full of chilly, snaking drafts. It must be cold enough outside to set up a differential, because this place didn't appear to be leaking like a sieve. Frankly, getting dressed was a pain these days, so he settled on shorts, boxers and a heavy flannel shirt that had been buried in his suitcase. Then he followed her to the kitchen.

She was wearing her terry cloth robe again, appearing cuddly, and looking through cabinets and her freezer.

"I'm eating everything, aren't I?" he asked.

"Not really. I just didn't know what you'd like to eat, and it didn't occur to me that I wouldn't be able to get to the store."

"Toast will do, if you have bread. Or peanut butter sandwiches."

She didn't answer immediately. He settled on a chair, propping his cane against the wall, and watched her lean back a little from her open fridge while she chewed her lower lip.

He had to fight not to just scoop her into his lap and get them both into some more trouble, but he was the guy who'd opened his yap about being hungry. Which was kind of ridiculous because he'd gone hungry for long periods. That particular gnawing in his stomach was just background.

Or had been until after the hospital. Maybe his body just kept demanding fuel for repairs. He guessed that wouldn't be surprising. Whatever, his appetite had mushroomed.

"When the weather clears tomorrow, I'll go out and buy something. I guess I've been eating you out of house and home."

"Hardly," she answered, glancing over her shoulder. "So you're not leaving as soon as the weather clears?"

"Not unless I get an invitation to."

She smiled before returning her attention to the contents of her refrigerator. "You won't get it from me."

Somehow he hadn't thought he would, although he seriously needed to think about what he was doing here. He didn't want to hurt this woman. He knew he was going to have to leave, for surgery, for rehab, maybe to return to the service. If he had a future, he didn't think it was here, although she made it very tempting. But no way was he going to depend on a woman, so he had to make himself independent.

He just didn't want to hurt her in the process.

But maybe it was already too late. He didn't think of himself as extraordinarily stupid, but maybe he had been this weekend. Where had his self-control gone? He'd depended on it his entire adult life.

Poof. Not cool.

She pulled a loaf of bread out of the freezer and tossed it on the counter. "For tomorrow," she said.

"It doesn't sound much calmer out there."

"No, it doesn't. I was sure it would be dying out tonight." The microwave clock said it was two in the morning. Already. This night was passing too fast, but emotionally, it felt like a lifetime. He'd experienced so much, felt so much in these hours with Miri. The only thing he could compare it to was the intensity of combat, and he didn't want to do that. He'd just enjoyed the most beautiful hours of his life. No comparisons there.

She closed the fridge. "If you can hang on a little while, I can make some muffins. Box mix."

"I don't want you going to so much trouble at this hour—"

She shook her head, silencing him. "I'm hungry, too, and nobody sleeps well hungry."

"We're going to sleep?" He loved the way she cracked up at that. He'd like to make her laugh like that all the time, but didn't seem the type of guy to cause much of that kind of laughter. Too sober and serious, at least until he had a few beers in him? Maybe.

God knew he laughed enough with his buddies when they were home and could hit a bar or have a barbecue in someone's yard. Knitted together in a way few would ever understand.

But since Al's death…well, he'd stopped laughing as much. Yeah, he'd lost men he cared about before, but Al had been unique. They'd gone through so much together over the years, shared so much experience, good and bad. He'd heard plenty of troops say they didn't bother to get to know the new guys because they wouldn't last long. Well, he and Al had never had that option. They'd been welded in training. While people had naturally come and gone over the years, he and Al had remained.

He suspected Al wouldn't like knowing he found it hard to laugh anymore. His friend wouldn't appreciate that at all.

Lost in memories, Gil was surprised when he realized that Miri was already popping a pan of muffins into the oven. Well, she'd said it would be easy, but it was impolite of him to have drifted away and left her alone while she did it.

But she didn't seem to mind. She came to the table and sat with her chin in her hand, looking drowsy. "Twenty minutes."

"Are you sure you don't just want to go to bed? I can take the muffins out of the oven, and you look ready to doze off."

"I'm feeling really good," she said, a sleepy smile on her face. "So relaxed. I don't want to snooze it away."

In the end, however, as soon as the muffins came out of the oven, without eating any, they went straight to bed. Sleep demanded its due, so curled together, they let it take them.

Morning came well before the sun, with an insistent ringing of Miri's phone. She lifted it off the cradle beside her bed, and without even opening her eyes, listened to the recorded message telling her that school was closed for the day.

Big surprise.

Gil, who had managed to roll onto his uninjured side and wrap an arm around her waist, mumbled, "It's too early, Teach."

"No kidding." She placed the receiver back into the cradle and, glancing at the clock, saw that it wasn't quite six yet. The sun wouldn't be up for a while, and since she had nowhere to go, she had no special desire to get up.

She sighed, loving the way Gil held her, enjoying his strength and warmth. Then, between one instant and the next, she fell into a sound sleep.

When she woke again, the sun still hadn't risen, but habit made her feel as if she were late. She was usually out her door and on her way to school at this time of year, when the sky was just beginning to lighten. She loved the experience of watching the day begin, then as spring drew closer, watching the sun rise earlier and earlier until it beat her to school.

She started to stir and heard Gil say, "Must you?"

"I must." The relaxation that had earlier filled her was beginning to transmute to anxiety. The storm would be over soon. Gil would be talking about moving on. Somehow, some way, she needed to put this night into a box for admiring but not touching.

She had to admit she felt weird as she rose, pulled on her robe and headed to the bathroom for her morning ablutions. Washing her face, brushing her teeth, debating whether the house was still too chilly to try to take another shower—these were ordinary things that didn't feel at all ordinary this morning.

She tossed Gil a smile as she emerged from the bathroom. He was sitting up against pillows, looking sharp-eyed now, watching her.

"I'll make some coffee." She headed down the hall to the kitchen, trying to pretend it was like any other morning in her life, making coffee, having a muffin for breakfast.

But it was not at all like any other night in her life,

and she knew it. She felt it all the way to her bones. Her world had been rocked and she didn't know if it would ever be able to settle into its familiar paths again.

Get over it, she told herself sternly. Sheesh, she'd been with the man for only three days. Everything before that had been secondhand from Al, or unrevealing from their emails. Gil couldn't have possibly made himself indelible so quickly, and she couldn't possibly be foolish enough at her age to turn all sappy over what was surely a one-night stand.

She had herself pretty well convinced by the time she heard Gil's uneven steps in the hallway. She'd be fine and could let him go.

The coffee started brewing, and she drew back the café curtain over the sink. "Oh, man," she said.

"What?" Gil asked from just behind her.

"There are two cars in my driveway. I know the sun isn't going to rise for a few more minutes, but right now all I can see are pink snowdrifts when the wind stops blowing."

She felt him come up behind her, instantly causing her every sense to grow sharp. She could smell him, a delightful scent of man mixed with lovemaking. She could feel his heat radiating from his body when he was still a short distance away. The sound of his uneven steps had become totally familiar, and now she couldn't imagine not hearing them.

She tried to pay attention to the cars, because they really were a sight. Then Gil, with the simple act of slipping an arm around her waist and leaning into her back, dropping a kiss on her neck, blew all resolutions to smithereens.

Then, as if nothing had happened, he said, "That's a lot of shoveling. I don't know how much I can help."

"You don't need to. There's a youngster down the street who likes to make a little pocket money by shoveling for me. If school weren't closed today, he'd probably have been here about the time I was getting the call."

The wind, though far less threatening than yesterday, still hadn't calmed completely. Zephyrs blew gently, but were strong enough to make the snow scatter like glitter in the brightening red light of dawn. Some larger flakes continued falling, but nothing like yesterday's whirlwind. The storm had nearly reached its end.

She felt him lean to one side before he spoke. "The roads look about the same. Buried. I thought I heard a plow in the wee hours."

"You might have. The wind defeats all comers. The snow we get here is usually pretty dry, and it blows and drifts forever. As bad as it was, if they were plowing it was for the sake of emergency vehicles."

She heard the hiss from the coffeepot, indicating it had finished. "Want some coffee and a muffin?"

"I'd like to stand right here like this with you forever, but I guess that's not possible."

She closed her eyes as his arm slipped away, feeling the loss of his touch as if skin were being ripped away. No, it wasn't possible. None of it was possible and she'd better wrap her head and heart around that. He'd never spoken a word to suggest that this hadn't been just a little friendly sex on a cold and miserable night when they both were probably feeling a bit lonely.

He got the mugs and small plates for the muffins. She brought the pot and the food to the table. As smoothly as if they'd been doing this for years.

But then there was no escaping it. Two people, virtual strangers, had just passed the most amazing night, as if a wedge had been cut out of time and set aside for their enjoyment, but then time flowed on as if it had never happened.

But it *had* happened and she wondered how she was going to deal with it all when he left. She wouldn't be able to slice out the memories.

He finished two muffins and was on his second cup of coffee when he at first said something innocuous. "Box mix or not, those were great blueberry muffins."

She crooked up one corner of her mouth. "You're just spoiled by military rations."

That drew a snort of laughter from him, but then his face sobered. "I didn't want to hurt you."

"What makes you think you have?" she retorted as her heart climbed into her throat. He was already regretting last night. She had a feeling it would be easier for her if he just walked out the door later today or tomorrow morning with a "See ya" rather than a discussion of the night past.

"I'm not fond of one-night stands or the women who are, and I'm pretty certain you're not one of them."

Something set her back up. She wasn't characteristically truculent, but she felt annoyance leap to the surface. "How would you know?" she demanded sharply. For as little as it was worth, she had the pleasure of seeing him taken aback. She hadn't thought that was in his repertoire of reactions. Granite man.

After nearly a minute, he replied. At first his tone was almost sarcastic, but quickly tapered into near gentleness. "Yeah, how would I know? I don't know you at all, really. Except you don't have that freaking hardened edge to you. You come at experience with a freshness I happen to like. Hell, I more than like it. You've reminded me the world can still hold beauty and innocence."

She caught her breath at that, stunned into silence. Did he really mean that?

"But I have to go," he said. "I've got one more family to visit, then I need to get back for my rehab and upcoming surgery."

At that her heart and stomach both began to sink, as if there was no bottom to the hole.

"Miri, I meant it when I said I don't want to hurt you. If Al were around, he'd kill me. So while I'm gone, I want you to think. We'll correspond—I might even get better at it now that I know you—and you can decide if you want me to come back this way."

She eyed him uncertainly. "You would need to decide, too."

He smiled. "I pretty much have. But I'd hate myself

if I didn't give you time to make up your mind without my persuasions."

She was going to miss his persuasions, but she knew deep within that he was absolutely right.

The blueberry muffin tasted like sawdust despite having been made with blueberries from the can, all nice and juicy, but she knew she needed to eat. Life must go on. She'd learned that the hard way. Her own mother, grief-stricken as she was, had forced food on her after her dad's death.

Just remember, Miri warned herself, he'd only said he'd come back this way. That meant next to nothing except friendship. She'd be foolish to count on anything more. And maybe he didn't mean anything at all. Maybe it was just a sop to her feelings, when all he wanted was to get away from here. From her. Making a semigraceful exit.

But then she found herself wondering just exactly what she wanted. Surely she didn't think she was in love already? She knew that this was hurting, a new kind of anguish. But why?

At last she stabilized her teetering emotions and managed a tight smile. "Still hungry? There are plenty more."

"No, thanks. They were great."

Then the anger began to bubble in place of the pain of impending loss. Yeah, and she'd been great last night, and she was a great woman with a lot to look forward to, and she couldn't possibly want to pursue a relationship with a broken-down soldier who couldn't even envision a future for himself.

Hell, she thought, rising with the plates, she could write his farewell speech for him. But she wondered how much of this had to do with Al. Did Gil feel he was betraying Al? Her thoughts were bouncing all over, while her heart ached, and anger tried to drive back the ache.

"Your timing stinks," she told him frankly, putting the plates and forks on the counter with a clatter. "We just had a great night together and you dump me before we finish breakfast?"

"Dump you?" He sounded startled.

"This is a kiss-off. For all I've had little experience, I can tell when I'm being told to get lost. Is this about Al?"

His voice came out a near growl. "Why would this be about Al?"

"Why wouldn't it be? You only came here because of him. You've spent more time here than you intended because of the storm. And here I was, the country girl who turned out to be easy pickings. Want me to write your farewell speech? Because I can."

"Miri…"

"Oh, shut up. You've said enough. Let the little lady down easy. Tell her you'll be back after you take care of important stuff. Tell her that she needs to think about it. Think about *what*, for Pete's sake? You haven't even been able to choke that out."

She turned to glare at him. "I don't have anything

to think about. There's nothing. We had some fun last night. That's it. It's done. No more."

She considered storming out, but then stayed as she was, feet planted, because she refused to act like a child. His expression had gone blank, like at the funeral, revealing nothing. The man of granite once more.

An eternity seemed to pass before he spoke again, his voice quiet and modulated. "While it may be true that I tried to stay in line because of Al, because I didn't want to take advantage of you, pretty soon nothing was about Al anymore. You crossed that chasm as if it wasn't there."

"Whee," she said, almost under her breath.

His flinty gray eyes met hers, holding her gaze and making her somehow unable to look away.

"Come off it," he said. "I trespassed. I'm willing to take any repercussions. What I don't want is to compound my sins here. There are so many things you don't know about me, and I don't just mean the things I'll never talk about. There are a whole lot of things I don't know about you. You just showed me you have a temper. That's something I didn't know about you. I like it, but, regardless, I didn't know, and there are probably a million more things I don't know. Most of them need years to discover, but right now we're still practically strangers."

She folded her arms, her eyes burning with tears she refused to shed, but anger kept her afloat. "Then why do I already feel like you're part of my life?"

He closed his eyes briefly. "For all you know, I could be a monster."

"True. But I doubt you'd have made it all these years in Uncle Sam's Army if you were. Nor would Al have liked you very much. You come with a sterling character reference. My cousin."

Gil swore softly and stood, grabbing his cane to lean on. "I'm trying to prevent a disaster here."

"Then when Lewis comes, I'll have him clear your car and your way out of here, and you can go. I don't want to be anyone's disaster."

As she spoke, the unmistakable roar of a plow sounded in the distance. It seemed to be heading this way.

"See?" she said. "You'll be able to escape soon."

Then, still angry and hurt, she tried to brush past him, but he snagged her with one arm, tight enough so that she couldn't twist away. In the next instant he'd sat down and pulled her onto his lap.

"Cut it out," he said softly.

She pushed on his shoulder with one hand. "Cut what out? Let me go."

"No." Just that one brief syllable.

"No?" She couldn't believe this. One minute he was telling her he was dumping her and the next she was imprisoned on his lap.

She pushed at him until she realized it was futile. All she could do was sit stiffly where she was. "What do you want?"

"For you to listen," he said bluntly. "You're an incredibly smart and talented person, so I'm sure if your feelings weren't getting in the way you'd realize that this is not a kiss-off and that I'm a lousy communicator when it comes to stuff like this. I can take a rebel-held cave, but I do a lousy job of talking about anything but strategy and tactics. So here I am, trying to run this like a military operation and everything is coming out sideways, and you can't read through the fog. I'm sorry."

She allowed herself to relax a hair. Besides, her outburst was beginning to embarrass her. She didn't usually act like that. In fact, it was rare. Man, had he gotten under her skin in a way almost no one did.

"I'm going to try again. We've been acquainted, mostly by email and through Al's stories, for a long time. But we only started to get to know each in real life on Friday. Today is Monday. That's not a very long time, Miri."

She hated to admit he was right. Last night had opened parts of her heart that she was quite sure had never opened before. Could that be illusion? Maybe.

He raised his hand and ran his fingers through her now-loose hair. A traitorous shiver ran through her.

"Last night was incredible," he continued. "No woman's ever made me feel as you have. It's important. I'll cherish it always. But is that firm ground on which to build? You know I'm already a bit messed up about my future. Do you want me to drag you into my mess just because of one fantastic night? Do you?"

She wanted so badly to say yes, but then she didn't

know exactly what he was talking about. Future friendship? Occasional flings? Something permanent? Oh, she hardly dared hope for that even though she yearned for it.

"The thing is," he continued, "I've never gone on a mission without meticulous planning."

"Which you said always blows up." Her voice was a little hoarse.

"True. But you need to know your goals and have some idea how to achieve them. So. Can I be blunt?"

"I thought you were."

He gave her a gentle squeeze. "I've been dancing around some things. Maybe I need to stop dancing. I think I love you, Miri. But I can't promise that after only three days. For the first time in my life you have me thinking about permanence, even though I try to avoid it. That's huge. And because it's so huge, we both need time. For all either of us knows, when I've been gone for a week you might be glad I'm not here. Let the intensity wane just a bit."

"So what do you want?" Her heart was racing again. It had started when he said he thought he loved her, then sped up even more when he mentioned permanence. Even so, she felt the niggle of uncertainty. He was right; they were still virtually strangers.

"Some time is all. I'll finish my surgery and rehab, we'll burn up the phone lines or video conference every night when possible, and we'll see. We'll see a whole lot better when you know if I'm asking you to pin yourself to a man who's going to be living halfway across the country because of his job, or if he can see his way to living here with a wonderful music teacher."

So he *was* talking forever. As in marriage. That *was* a huge decision, and she was keenly aware that it shouldn't be made in a rush. And as he'd just reminded her, there was so much uncertainty still to be resolved. The tight band around her chest began to ease a little. Not hopeless. It wasn't hopeless.

Then he caught her chin in his hand and tipped her face so that he could kiss her deeply and passionately, until she clung to him, nearly breathless.

When he lifted his head, she opened her eyes to see his face.

"Dammit, woman," he said, "I'm asking for a long engagement."

That word settled it and made everything crystal clear for her. Anger and pain fell away before a burst of joy. *Engagement.*

"Yes," she whispered. "Oh, yes."

His smile was amazing, so bright and free of shadows. He nuzzled her lips with his.

"The campaign," he said, "begins now."

She could hardly wait.

Epilogue

Miri realized that she had lost the attention of her marching band. They still stood on the grassy field in front of her, beneath a cloudless sky in a soft, warm breeze that ruffled their tees and shorts, but they certainly weren't looking at her. They looked past her toward the school parking lot.

She turned to see what had their attention before calling them to order. Her heart lodged in her throat.

Gil York, in full dress uniform, looking as he had at Al's funeral, was watching from the edge of the field. She gaped at the sight.

"Don't mind me," he called. "Just a spectator."

Giggles ran through the band, letting her know that not all of them quite believed that. Why not? At the moment she hardly cared. A glance at her watch told her they had twenty minutes left before parents would arrive to pick up their kids.

But Gil's presence had diverted her, just as it had her students. She hadn't expected him, although lately they'd been talking more and more about him coming to visit, about a long-term future together.

But without warning? She tried to key in on where they were in the process of learning their marching patterns and where she wanted to go from here.

The band's formation had started to get a little sloppy. Girls were whispering to each other and eyeing Gil as if he were a cake.

The beginning of the school year was always hardest. These students hadn't even started their classroom semester. They showed up for these camps because it was a requirement for those who wanted to be in the marching band.

"Dress right," she called out. "Straighten out those ranks."

Before long, they'd feel the entire performance. Their steps would come naturally and they wouldn't have to keep checking one another to make sure they were in the right place. But first they had to get all this correct more than once, and they were just beginning. By the first football game, they'd be impressive.

So she walked them through another ten minutes of evolutions, then had to follow everyone into the band room. Instruments needed to be put away in their cages or packed up to go home for practice, and she had to make sure that the last band member's parent had arrived to take him or her home.

It felt like everything had slowed down to sludge. Her mind was silently ordering her students to hurry it up, even though they were having their usual relaxed gab sessions as they put everything away. All she wanted to do was see Gil.

She could hardly maintain her usual composure. Impatience was swamping her, but at last the final student walked out the door. Just as she picked up a few items from the floor and prepared to turn out the lights, she heard Gil.

"Miri."

She turned slowly, a piece of crumpled paper in her hand. "Tell me it's not another funeral," she said, indicating his uniform. God, he looked good in it. Her mouth was growing dry and she reached for a bottle of water on the corner of her desk, making herself swallow, making herself wait.

"It's not a funeral. And look, no cane." He held out his arms.

Her throat tightened. He'd come to tell her he was going back on active duty, and then she'd have to decide whether to follow him or stay here or… "That's truly great news," she said honestly, even though his unannounced visit was raising unpleasant specters in her mind.

"Stop catastrophizing," he said. He closed the distance between them and drew her into his arms. "I've waited so long for this," he whispered. "So long."

Every other thing in the world flew from her mind as they kissed, as she nearly tried to burrow into his strength.

"I love you," he said, lifting his head. "I truly love you, and I don't care what I have to do, we're going to make this work. Unless you don't—"

"Oh, I do," she said swiftly, without any lingering doubt. Her heart felt as if he'd just filled it with helium and it was rising into the sky. "I love you, Gil. I love you, love you, love you, and I've missed you so much every single minute of every day."

He smiled down into her eyes. "I have choices, Miri, and some of them involve staying here in Conard County. We can discuss that later. What I want to know is will you marry this broken soldier and make him the happiest man on earth?"

Her heart sang. "Yes. Absolutely."

"Kids, too?" he asked.

"Kids, too." Then she leaned into him, letting him surround her with his power and strength.

She thought of Al, suspected he'd wanted to encourage this and decided he must be feeling smug right then.

But an instant later she forgot everything else except the man who held her and had just promised her the best of all possible futures.

* * * * *

COMING NEXT MONTH FROM

HARLEQUIN®

SPECIAL EDITION

Available February 20, 2018

#2605 THE FORTUNE MOST LIKELY TO...
The Fortunes of Texas: The Rulebreakers • by Marie Ferrarella

Everett Fortunado has never quite gotten over his high school love, Lila Clark. So when circumstance offers him a second chance, he grabs it. But is Lila willing to forget their past and risk her heart on a millionaire doctor with ties to the Fortunes?

#2606 THE SHERIFF'S NINE-MONTH SURPRISE
Match Made in Haven • by Brenda Harlen

After a weekend of shared passion, Katelyn Gilmore doesn't expect to see Reid Davidson again—until she meets Haven's new sheriff! But she has a surprise, too—scheduled to arrive in nine months...

#2607 A PROPOSAL FOR THE OFFICER
American Heroes • by Christy Jeffries

Fighter pilot Molly Markham is used to navigating her own course. Billionaire Kaleb Chatterson has never found a problem he couldn't fix. But when the two pretend to be in a fake relationship to throw off their families, neither one has control over their own hearts.

#2608 THE BEST MAN TAKES A BRIDE
Hillcrest House • by Stacy Connelly

Best man Jamison Porter doesn't believe in a love of a lifetime. But will his daughter's adoration of sweet—and sexy—wedding planner Rory McClaren change this cynical lawyer's mind about finding a new happily-ever-after?

#2609 FOREVER A FATHER
The Delaneys of Sandpiper Beach • by Lynne Marshall

After a devastating loss, Daniel Delaney just wants to be left alone with his grief and his work. But his new employee, the lovely Keela O'Mara, and her daughter might be just the people to help remind him that love—and family—can make life worth living again.

#2610 FROM EXES TO EXPECTING
Sutter Creek, Montana • by Laurel Greer

When Tavish Fitzgerald, a globe-trotting photojournalist, gets stuck in Montana for a family wedding, one last night with Lauren Dawson, his hometown doctor ex-wife, leads them from exes to expecting—and finally tempts him to stay put!

Get 2 Free Books,
Plus 2 Free Gifts —
just for trying the Reader Service!

SPECIAL EXCERPT FROM

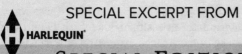

HARLEQUIN®

SPECIAL EDITION

*Everett Fortunado never got over his high school love,
Lila Clark. So when circumstance offers him a second
chance, he grabs it with both hands. But is Lila willing
to forget their past and risk her heart on a millionaire
doctor with ties to the Fortunes?*

Read on for a sneak preview of
THE FORTUNE MOST LIKELY TO...
by USA TODAY bestselling author
Marie Ferrarella, *the next installment in*
THE FORTUNES OF TEXAS:
THE RULEBREAKERS *continuity.*

Before Lila could ask any more questions, she suddenly
found herself looking up at Everett. The fund-raiser was
a black-tie affair and Everett was wearing the obligatory
tuxedo.

It was at that moment that Lila realized Everett in a tuxedo
was even more irresistible than Everett wearing scrubs.

Face it, the man would be irresistible even wearing a kilt.

"What are you doing here?" Lila asked when she finally
located her tongue and remembered how to use it.

"You know, we're going to have to work on getting you
a new opening line to say every time you see me," Everett
told her with a laugh. "But to answer your question, I was
invited."

Lucie stepped up with a slightly more detailed explanation
to her friend's question. "The invitation was the foundation's
way of saying thank you to Everett for his volunteer work."

"Disappointed to see me?" he asked Lila. There was a touch of humor in his voice, although he wasn't quite sure just what to make of the stunned expression on Lila's face.

"No, of course not," Lila denied quickly. "I'm just surprised, that's all. I thought you were still back in Houston."

"I was," Everett confirmed. "The invitation was express mailed to me yesterday. I thought it would be rude to ignore it, so here I am," he told her simply, as if all he had to do was teleport himself from one location to another instead of drive over one hundred and seventy miles.

"Here you are," Lila echoed.

Everything inside her was smiling and she knew that was a dangerous thing. Because when she was in that sort of frame of mind, she tended not to be careful. And that was when mistakes were made.

Mistakes with consequences.

She was going to have to be on her guard, Lila silently warned herself. And it wasn't going to be easy being vigilant, not when Everett looked absolutely bone-meltingly gorgeous the way he did.

As if his dark looks weren't already enough, Lila thought, the tuxedo made Everett look particularly dashing.

You're not eighteen anymore, remember? Lila reminded herself. *You're a woman. A woman who has to be very, very careful.*

She just hoped she could remember that.

Don't miss
THE FORTUNE MOST LIKELY TO...
by Marie Ferrarella, available March 2018 wherever
Harlequin® Special Edition books and ebooks are sold.

www.Harlequin.com